I0587368

HONEYMOON HEARSAY

PET WHISPERER P.I.
BOOK 17

MOLLY FITZ

ABOUT THIS BOOK

The old stone mansion Charles and I have booked for our week-long honeymoon seems to be something straight out of a fairytale.

That is, until it all starts to fall apart. *Quite literally.* My poor husband plunges straight through the staircase on our first night--and it's a real wonder he didn't need serious medical intervention after that.

I want to find another place to stay, but Charles insists he's okay and that he'd like to see the week out. Of course, we become stucker than stuck when we stumble upon a lost kitten crying for her missing mama in the back garden.

We can't just leave her, but we also can't stay here, especially once deadly rumors begin buzzing in the garden... What happened to Charles wasn't a mistake, but he also may not be the intended target.

Time to find the kitten's mama and skedaddle. I just got married; I'm definitely not ready to become a widow!

My name is Angie Longfellow. Yup, it's official as of the day before yesterday. I'm a married woman, who is currently headed toward a luxury honeymoon destination with new hubby at her side.

I still can't believe it really happened.

Getting married is probably the most normal thing I've done with my life, yet it also feels like the biggest adventure so far.

And that's saying something, considering I racked up seven associate degrees as I struggled with academic indecision, started my own business as a private investigator, and can secretly talk to animals.

Oh, you're wondering about that last part? Well, allow me to explain...

It all started with a will reading at the law firm where I used to work as a paralegal. The same law firm where I met my new husband—*eep!*—but I digress.

As a glorified secretary, it was my job to make the coffee. The partners hadn't sprung for new appliances in quite some time, and the coffee maker was more than a little worse for wear. When I tried to plug it in, the darned thing zapped me unconscious.

I woke up a short bit later to the smell of tuna and the sound of someone addressing me in a very conde-scending manner. I didn't know it then, but that someone was the deceased's beloved cat Octavius. He told me his owner had been murdered and that he needed help to prove it and thus get justice for the old lady he'd loved so dearly.

If you know cats as well as I do, then you know that Mr. Octavius refused to take "no" for an answer. With no choice but to comply, a partnership was born.

We solved the murder together and became friends while doing it. I was asked to adopt him by the estate's trustee, and I eagerly agreed—even before I knew a certain tabby had a generous trust fund attached to him.

I took to calling him Octo-Cat, and together we

moved into his former owner's enormous manor house at his behest. Now the two of us are partners in crime... make that partners in *solving crimes*. Yes, we run the P.I. business together. We don't always agree, but one way or another, we always get the job done.

And it's because of my strange ability to speak with animals that I really got to know my new husband, Charles. He overheard me trying to sneak in a FaceTime call with Octo-Cat at work—and proceeded to use this knowledge to blackmail me into helping with a difficult case he'd just landed.

That all worked out too, even though honestly he could have just politely asked for my help rather than resorting to blackmail. I already had a huge crush on him and would have jumped at any excuse to spend more time together. And time is all we have on our lengthy two-day drive from Maine to Virginia.

My mom and dad managed to book a gorgeous private mansion for our honeymoon, and we'll have the entire place to ourselves for a whole week to usher in our era of newly wedded bliss. It's the same place they honeymooned more than thirty years ago, which bodes well for us, seeing as the two of them are still crazy in love.

I'll miss everyone while we're away for the week, but I know Nan will keep everyone back home in check. Lucky for her, she won't be able to understand all the complaints Octo-Cat and Charles's two hairless cats, Jacques and Jillianne, are sure to send her way. She'll also have her sweet rescue dog Paisley to keep her company and her brand-new surprise husband Grant, along with his Holland Lop bunny EB. It's a full house for sure!

I'm sure I'll still call at least once per day to play translator and mediator for whatever problems arise, but it's nothing my scrappy grandmother can't handle... Provided our resident raccoon Pringle behaves himself. Lately he's been turning over a new leaf with the help of a certain twelve-step program, and we recently shared a very heartfelt bonding moment, but his natural tendencies still encourage him to gossip and thieve whenever possible.

But no, I'm sure it will all be fine—just fine.

I need to stop worrying about everyone we left in Maine and focus on the wonderful week in Virginia ahead. It's my honeymoon, and my new husband deserves my full attention. It will probably be good for me to have this little break from all the drama and chaos of the busy household back home. I can put out any fires when I return next week.

This week is all about celebrating my new marriage, and that's exactly what I plan to focus on.

* * *

"Look at the trees," I remarked, pointing out the side window as Charles and I entered the final hour of our big road trip. We were getting very close to the old stone mansion where we'd be spending the next week, and I was jittery with excitement. "They're changing."

"We've got a long way until autumn," he answered while fiddling with the radio.

I shook my head and pointed again. "No, like they're a completely different type. We don't have trees like this back in Blueberry Bay."

"Touché." He laughed. "Leave it to you to notice the forest *and* the trees."

"You can take the detective out of the agency..." I laughed too. "But no sleuthing this week. Promise."

I grabbed Charles's hand from the radio while he used the other to guide the steering wheel. "The next seven days are about you and me, and only you and me."

"I like the sound of that," he said flirtatiously before raising our linked hands to kiss the back of mine. "And we're almost there. Our turn-off is in less than thirty miles, and from there it's a straight shot to our little Southern slice of paradise."

"So what should we do first once we get there?"

"Oh, I think you know, Mrs. Longfellow." He glanced toward me for a second, then winked before returning his gaze to the highway.

Heat rushed to my cheeks. I was still very new at being a wife and not yet comfortable with all the intricacies that came with the role. Especially with talking about them.

So I redirected the conversation a little bit. "I mean, *after*? I've been reading about the area on Trip Advisor. There are all kinds of historical tours, and some really nice restaurants, and..."

Charles squeezed my hand. "This is our honeymoon. It's not about seeing the sights. Let's just relax and enjoy each other's company."

I wriggled in my seat. "Relax, right. I can do that."

He chuckled good-naturedly. "Yes, you can. If your workaholic husband can enjoy some time off the grid, then so can you. Besides, we'll have each other, and that's all we really need, right?"

"Right," I said, nodding my head sharply, which only sent us both into another fit of giggles. "This week is only about us, but we can still try some of the local restaurants, right? I might die if I don't get true authentic Southern-made biscuits and gravy for breakfast at least once this week."

"Of course! We'll have them every day if you'd like. We'll need something to keep up our stamina between... well, you know."

I blushed like mad at the implication and tried to hide my hot cheeks behind my palms.

"Oh, Angie Longfellow, I love you. Never change," my husband said before releasing my hand to casually rub my shoulder.

Never change. Now that I could do. But could I avoid all my usual worries and busy-bodying for one whole week?

I guess time would tell on that one.

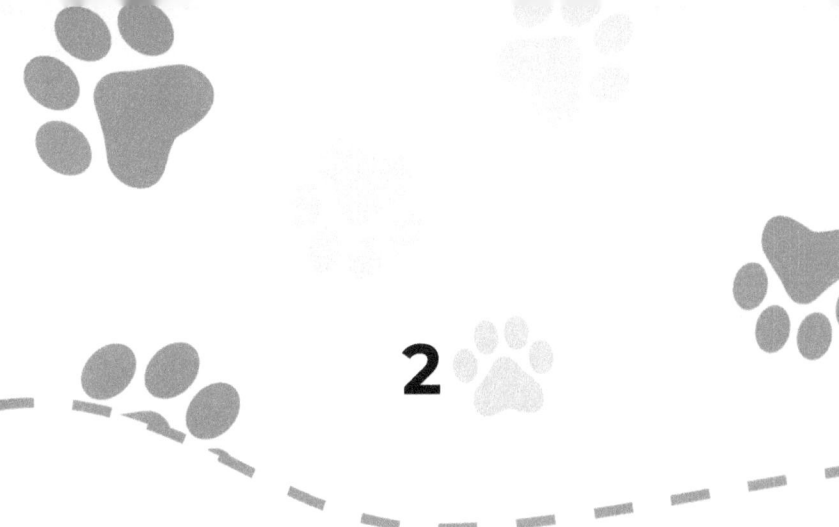

2

"There it is!" I exclaimed as the old stone mansion loomed into view. Even though we split the trip into two days, we'd still driven a long way to reach our destination, and now that we were here, I couldn't wait to get out and stretch my legs a bit.

"Are you sure this is the place?" Charles slowed the car to a crawl as we both gawked at the property ahead. "There seem to be a lot of cars, and we're supposed to have the place to ourselves."

I waved off his concern with a quick sweep of my hand. "I'm sure it's just the staff getting it ready for us. Make sure you give them a nice tip, so it's not awkward."

"Right, okay." He pulled into the small gravel lot

beside the mansion and parked next to an old truck, then took out his wallet and thumbed through it for some cash, which he tucked in his front pocket so it would be ready.

I squealed as I hopped out of the car. "*Eee!* I can't believe we're really here."

Charles climbed out of the driver's seat and popped the trunk so we could grab our luggage. "Well, believe it. Only the best for my wifey."

I wheeled one large suitcase behind me while Charles balanced two overstuffed duffle bags. "Look at this garden. It's even more beautiful than my mom described. Is that hydrangea? Look how big and puffy!"

"We can eat your biscuits and gravy out here and watch the sunrise. Want to try for tomorrow?"

"That sounds great, honey, but tomorrow, I'm sleeping in. Let's do it the day after, though, for sure." When I turned back to look at Charles, I delighted in the enormous smile that decorated his handsome face.

"I can't believe the size of this place," he noted, eyeing the mansion. I turned back to study the domicile in all its refinement and grandeur. It appeared to be a mishmash of architectural styles, landing somewhere between a Scottish castle and a Colonial.

Whoever had ordered this house to be built clearly had a very creative mind. I wouldn't be surprised if we ran across a few trap doors or secret passages during our stay. I couldn't wait to explore.

We reached the doorstep and paused to collect ourselves. I tucked a loose strand of hair behind my ear as I studied the bright green front door. "I guess we just knock? Or do we head right in? Mom didn't have any information about a key exchange, and I couldn't find this place on Airbnb when I looked."

Charles stepped forward, cleared his throat, and thumped on the door.

And someone pulled it open almost immediately, a little old lady with blue hair and thick glasses. She smiled at us, then turned toward the interior of the house and shouted, "Billy, the honeymooners are here!"

A middle-aged man with a pot belly shuffled out and grabbed my suitcase, leaving Charles to handle his own duffle bags. I stood on tiptoe to kiss my husband's cheek in excitement. "This is it! The place is all ours!"

"What was that, dearie?" the old lady shouted my way.

"Oh, sorry. We're just excited to have free rein of

this gorgeous house for the whole week," I explained with an awkward smile.

"You don't exactly have free rein," the man whom she'd called Billy informed us. "The third floor and attic are off limits to guests, and obviously you'll need to keep to your room or the communal places on the property."

"Wait. *Our room?*" I squeaked, not knowing what else to say.

Charles immediately jumped into lawyer mode. "I think there may be some misunderstanding. This is our honeymoon, and my wife's parents expressly reserved the entire property for the week as a gift to us."

"There's no misunderstanding on our end," the old woman piped up, taking her glasses off to clean them on the hem of her shirt. "Costs a lot of money to maintain a place like this, especially since it belongs to the official register of historical homes in the area. And that garden? Quality gardeners don't come cheap, dearie."

My heart sank as I filled in the blanks. "So you turned it into a B&B to help pay the bills?"

"About five years back now. Your mother hasn't been for a while, I'm guessing. I can't believe she assumed she was reserving the whole place for the cost of a single room. Ha!" She hunched over and slapped her knee.

"There are no refunds without at least two weeks' notice, so you're out of time. Do you want your room or not?" Billy sniffed indifferently.

I looked to Charles for a decision since we obviously weren't going to be offered any privacy to discuss our options.

"We want it," he said decisively, shooting me a meaningful look that I had a hard time deciphering just then.

Billy nodded and headed toward a narrow staircase. "Very well. Let me show you the way."

We followed the man up the stairs to a locked door at the far end of the hall. "You only get the one room, but it's our best room," he offered almost apologetically as he turned a key in the lock and pushed the door open.

And immediately I gasped as I took in the oversized canopy bed and soft lace curtains. The entire room was something out of a time capsule, transporting us straight to the early days of our nation and showing how the one percent lived in ornate luxury. Blue flowered vines danced along the wallpaper, and the honey oak hardwood floors appeared to be original. Best of all, a stone fireplace sat opposite the bed with a gorgeous antique love seat positioned comfortably before it.

"Nice, huh?" Billy grunted as he tossed my suitcase onto the bed.

"I love it," I confessed as I turned in a circle to take it all in.

"Thanks for your help," Charles said, shaking our guide's hand and probably slipping some money into it for a sly tip.

"Dinner's at eight p.m. sharp. It's included in the cost of your package, if you want to join us."

This caught my attention. "What's on the menu?"

"No menu. This isn't a restaurant." He narrowed his eyes at me, leaving no doubt the hospitality industry was not Billy's first choice for a career. "We all eat the same, so if you're gluten-free, nut-free, dairy-free, or meat-free, you're free to go grab your grub elsewhere. If you're not too fussy, then you'll love Madame Blue's cooking."

I blinked back my surprise at the way he delivered this invitation. "Madame Blue? Is that...?"

"Yup, you already met her downstairs. She's a much better cook than she is greeter. That's why she keeps me around."

Right, because Billy here was the paragon of hospitality.

"Okay, thanks again." Charles moved toward the door.

Thankfully, the other man took the hint and followed. "The name's Bill. If you need anything, just give a holler."

I smiled and waved goodbye right before Bill took his leave and thumped the door closed behind him.

Charles turned toward me with a bemused expression. "So things are a little different than we expected," he prompted with a sigh. "I figured we should at least take it for now, so we have a private place to discuss our options. I'd be happy to go somewhere else, if you'd rather."

"Honestly, it's fine. You wanted to spend most of our time in the room anyway, right?" I sank down onto the bed and patted the mattress beside me. "Now get over here, Mr. Longfellow."

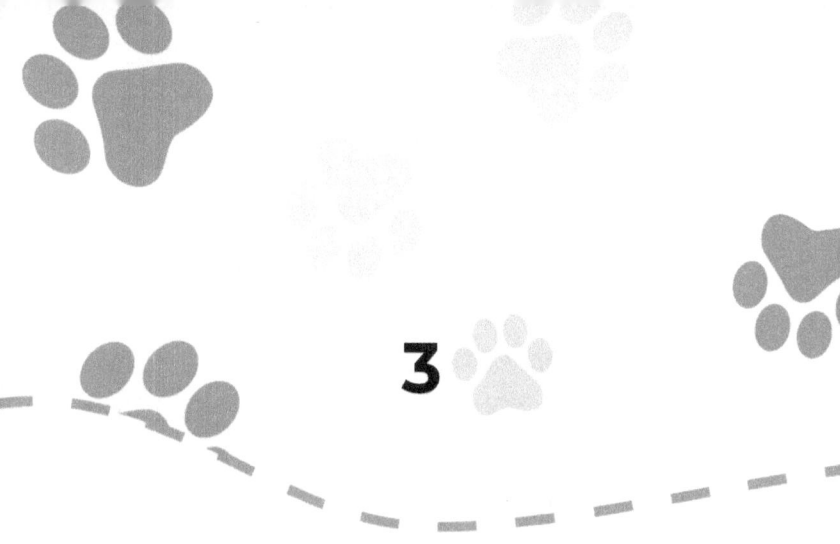

3

After a bit of time to ourselves, Charles and I decided to take a look around the garden. We headed outside hand in hand, swinging our arms between us as we strolled up to a pair of stone cupid statues that stood amid a bed of bright yellow roses.

"I should do more with our yard back home," I said, stooping down to breathe in the sweet fragrance, startled when a fat bee buzzed out from between the petals. I jolted back, hoping I hadn't already upset the creature.

"Oof, careful. I'm allergic to bees!" Charles cried, taking a giant step back and waving his arms about.

"Really? How did I not know that?" I cocked my head to the side as I studied him.

"Because we don't have any gardens back home. Probably best to keep it that way too."

"Better bees than shellfish, I guess. Octo-Cat would never forgive you if we had to stop getting his favorite lobster rolls from Little Dog Diner." I smiled thinking of my crabby tabby back home. Darn it, I missed him already. "Do you want to go back inside?"

Charles shook his head. "I'm not deathly allergic. Well, not unless I get stung by a whole hive. My wife wants to enjoy the gardens, so let's enjoy the gardens. I'll just take some Benadryl when we go back inside, and worst case, I have an EpiPen tucked into the front pocket of my duffle."

"An EpiPen?" I frowned as I looked up at him. "That sounds pretty serious."

"Just a precaution. You know me, always prepared like some kind of overgrown Boy Scout." Charles caught my look of horror and backtracked quickly. "I'm fine. I promise. Look, there are those hydrangeas you saw coming in." He pointed and took off toward the puffy pink flower balls.

I shook my head and followed. Why was he only confiding this allergy in me now?

Mom had spent most of her time describing the beautiful landscaping when she told us about this place. At least that hadn't changed, even if the larger establishment had.

Grassy paths guided us through the generous display of collected plant life. We saw so much diversity in size, color, and type, I seemed to find a new favorite every time the winding path led us to a new bed of blooms.

As we approached the red brick wall that flanked the property, I had a thought that caused me to pull out my phone and do a quick web search. I paused to read through the information on the screen while Charles continued to wander ahead.

A few minutes later, I glanced up ready to share my findings, but my husband was nowhere to be seen. "Charles?" I called, craning my neck to search the area.

"Over here," he called softly, popping up from the ground and waving his hand.

I wasted no time striding right on over. "There are all kinds of non-pollinating flowers." I revealed the fruit of my research labors as I walked swiftly his way. "We can still have a garden, as long as we're careful about what we—"

"Shhh," Charles said, raising a finger to his lips then pointing toward the ground.

I fell quiet, moving as fast as I could to see what

this was all about. As I drew closer, his wide smile grew in size.

"Do you see it?" he whispered and pointed toward a patch of clover near the brick wall.

I narrowed my eyes just in time to see a tiny black paw stretch into the air. "Is that—?"

"A kitten," he confirmed, squatting back down to watch it sleep.

"What's it doing out here?" I demanded, even though he clearly didn't know, either. "Do you think it's a stray?"

He reached his fingers forward carefully and scratched at the little white patch of fur on the sleeping kitten's chest. "No idea. You could ask it though."

Now there was a thought, but still I hesitated. "Are you sure you don't mind? I thought we were both leaving work back home."

"Your bond with animals is a part of who you are. It's not something you can turn on and off at will. Besides, I want to know what he's doing here, too."

"Not he. *She*. It's a girl," I clarified, watching that fuzzy little chest rise and fall with each breath.

"How can you tell?" He looked from me to the kitten and back again.

"I don't know. I just can. Should I wake her up to say hello?"

He pushed himself back to standing. "Go ahead. I'll keep watch to make sure no one stumbles by and gets curious."

"Good idea," I murmured, but Charles had already moved to the end of the nearest path, giving me and the kitten some time to ourselves.

Despite the saying being to let sleeping dogs lie, I normally knew better than to wake a cat. Octo-Cat had taught me that lesson the hard way—and many times over at that. But this kitten seemed so small, and it could very well need our help. As a baby, hopefully it didn't have the same reserve of colorful kitty curses to call upon.

I placed a hand gently on its side and felt a rumbling purr through my fingers. That was an encouraging sign.

"Hello, little one," I said softly, waiting for any form of response. But the kitty remained fast asleep.

I stroked her fur softly. "Hi. My name is Angie, and I'm a friend," I continued, applying increasing pressure with my strokes to wake her gently.

Finally, two little yellow eyes blinked open. "Where's my mommy?" the baby mewled, and I swear my heart broke in two.

"Hi there, sleepyhead. I can help you find your mommy. Where did you last see her?"

The kitten remained lying on her side. She looked weak. "She told me to wait by the fence, but she hasn't come back. It's been a really long time."

"Do you have any brothers or sisters? Are they around here somewhere, too?" I was already going into full-on rescue mode. Thankfully, I knew Charles would want to help the baby, too. After all, he was the one who'd discovered her.

The kitten drew in a deep breath before answering. "It's just me and my mommy now. My brothers and sisters got taken inside a house by a nice lady while Mommy was off hunting. I was scared so I hid."

"You don't have to be scared of me," I offered with what I hoped was a kind smile. I made sure to only use closed-lip smiles with animals, since the sight of teeth often sent them on the defensive. "And we'll look for your mommy together. But before we do, are you hungry?"

This got the kitten to rise to her feet and perform a series of stretches. "Yes, very much so."

"Then let's go see if Madame Blue has some milk she can share," I said, impressing myself with my ability to remember the old lady's name after hearing it only once. "Before we go inside, though, would you tell me your name?"

"My name is Charlene," she answered around a yawn as she finished her stretches. "And my mommy's name is Mommy. I really miss her. Do you think we'll find her soon?"

"I'm going to do everything I can to help you find her, but first let's get some food in you. You'll feel better once your tummy's full."

The kitty nodded. "Okay."

"Do you mind if I carry you to the house?" I asked. Charlene had clearly been born a stray, and I didn't want to frighten her by picking her up without first getting permission.

"Okay, but please be gentle," she squeaked.

I leaned down and carefully lifted her into my arms. She was so tiny, she could practically fit on the palm of my hand. "It's okay. I've got you now, and I won't rest until I know you're safe."

wasted no time introducing Charles to the kitten he'd found sleeping in the garden. "Hi, Charles. This is Charlene. She's lost her mother, but we're going to help her find her."

"Oh, of course, we are," Charles cooed, running his knuckles over the kitty's head the way his Sphynx cats liked.

"What is he doing?" Charlene cried, pressing herself into my chest.

"He's just saying hello," I assured her. "Charles is my husband. He's the one who found you."

She scrunched up her nose as she considered this. "Why is his name like my name?"

I chuckled. "I don't know. I guess that's just a fun coincidence, but shhh. We're heading into the house now, and I won't be able to talk to you once we're inside."

"Why not?"

"Because most other humans can't talk to cats. They'll think it's weird and get scared if they hear us talking to each other. And we don't want to cause a scene. We just want to get you fed and then find your mommy, okay?"

Charlene appeared to think about this for a moment before letting go of some of the tension in her tiny body and saying, "Okay. I'll be quiet."

I reached down to stroke her head as Charles pushed open the front door. "I think the kitchen's back there," I told him, heading decisively to the right.

"I thought you said not to talk," the kitten cried out.

"Hush, little baby," I cooed like a mother singing a lullaby. The only time I could get away with talking to animals in the presence of those who didn't know my secret was when using a cutesy baby voice to say very basic things—the way most people did with their pets, not expecting them to be able to talk back. Charlene didn't know this, but I hoped my words would soothe her all the same.

Sure enough, she said nothing more and we found

the kitchen easily. The old woman Charles and I had met earlier now sported an apron tied around her slim hips as she began to work on that night's supper.

"No guests in the kitchen!" she shouted upon noticing us.

The kitten shrunk back in my hands, but I strode forward with confidence. "Sorry to trouble you. We found this little one outside in the garden, and she seems to be missing her mother. I was hoping we could have a spot of milk to offer her. She appears to be quite hungry."

"No pets are allowed on the property," was her only reply. She didn't even bother looking at the poor needy creature.

I refused to give up. Surely this woman had an ounce of kindness somewhere in her cranky soul. "She's not a pet. We just found her outside, and she's very hungry. Could we please have that milk, if you don't mind?"

"*I do mind.* The historical society is just looking for any reason to remove me as caretaker, and the last thing I need is guest complaints about little black hairs in their dinners. Now shoo!" Madame Blue used her small body to force us back toward the doorway, waving a wire whisk at us to really get her point across.

"Well, that didn't go great," I said, letting out a breath of frustration.

"I'll run into town and grab some supplies. Do you want to stay here with Charlene?" my husband offered helpfully once we were out of earshot of the kitchen.

"She said no pets allowed on the premises," I reminded him with a pout, but he was undeterred.

"Well, good thing Charlene isn't a pet." He reached out to rub his knuckles over her head again, and this time the kitten leaned into him. "She's just a friend we're helping out. Probably best you keep her hidden though."

"Thank you." I leaned in to hug him. "Will you be able to make it there and back by dinner, though?"

He checked the time on his phone and frowned. "Probably not. You go down without me. I'll feed Charlene once I'm back with the supplies, then I'll come down and join you. I'll grab some snacks while I'm out too, just in case Madame Blue's cooking is terrible."

"Right?" I smirked at his sneaky jibe. "I thought the special ingredient in Southern cooking was supposed to be love. She definitely missed that memo."

"It will be fine," he assured me, stroking the kitten

lovingly while I held her. "If our host is still being horrible by the time we find Charlene's mother, we can book the rest of the week somewhere else, okay?"

I smiled at that. I loved how little he let these kinds of setbacks bother him. "Okay," I agreed with a huge smile. "Now give me a kiss goodbye before you go."

My husband happily obliged this request. "Now get upstairs quick," he urged, pushing me toward the narrow staircase. "Before that crotchety old lady comes back out to yell at you again."

Well, I didn't need to be told twice. I jogged up the stairs, taking extra care not to jostle my precious cargo as I went. Once inside our room, I locked the door behind me and set Charlene on the plush bedspread.

"This should be a more comfortable place to nap for now. Do you want me to stay here with you, or go outside to see if I can find your mommy?"

Charlene glanced around the room with a shiver. "I don't want to be alone. Will you stay?"

"Of course I'll stay." I smiled at the sleepy baby as she explored the large bed and finally curled up on one of the pillows with her tail tucked tight around her body.

"Will you tell me a story?" she asked, a bit more

upbeat now that she'd gotten comfortable. "Mommy always told me stories before I go to sleep."

"Sure, uh..." I racked my brain for a story that a young feline might enjoy. "Oh, I've got it! Once upon a time there was a very spoiled cat named Octavius."

Charlene stretched her paws before her. "Is this a true story?"

I bobbed my head enthusiastically. "Yes, it's very true. It's about my very best friend in the whole world. He's waiting back home while Charles and I are on our honeymoon."

"What's a honeymoon?" she asked, tilting her head to one side.

"It's like a special vacation two people take after they get married."

"I don't know a lot of the words you use, but I like the sound of your voice," Charlene said with a twitch of her whiskers.

I chuckled softly. "Should I keep going with the story? I can try to use easier words."

"No, I like hearing the new words. They make me smarter, right?"

"Definitely."

"So use all the biggest words you know, and I promise not to interrupt again."

"Okay, here goes…" I paused to make sure she was ready and listening.

Charlene's wide, unblinking eyes focused on me. Time to shine.

"Once there was an incredibly pampered feline by the name of Octavius," I continued, using a dramatic old-time voice. "Octavius believed himself to be the most exquisite cat who ever lived and often told others of his greatness. For the longest time, nobody understood his not-so-humble boasts, but one day, thanks to a shoddy coffee maker, he met a human woman who did understand…"

I let my voice fade away when I noticed that Charlene had already fallen fast asleep. I sat and watched her for a little while, debating the urge to go search the gardens for her mother while I had a bit of free time. But by then, it was fast approaching eight o'clock, and even though I didn't look forward to any more interactions with the unfriendly caretaking duo, I couldn't deny the way my stomach grumbled upon smelling the delicious blend of savory scents that wafted up the stairs from the kitchen.

Charles would be back soon to leave a saucer of milk and some soft food for our little visitor, which meant she wouldn't be alone for long—and she'd wake to a nice meal waiting for her.

Now it was time to see about a nice meal to fill my own belly. I just hoped the food would be worth the uncomfortable conversation that would surely be accompanying it.

5

I wandered into the dining room five minutes before eight, not wanting to risk upsetting Blue or Billy by being late. I was the first to arrive in the gorgeous dining room that came equipped with a mahogany table to seat at least twelve situated beneath a stunning crystal chandelier.

Charles and I had only checked in a few hours prior but hadn't happened upon any other guests during that time, leaving me to wonder if we were the only ones here besides the staff. I couldn't decide whether that would be a good thing or a bad one. Other guests meant that the rude caretakers would be less fixated on us, but it also meant more people who might intrude upon moments Charles and I preferred to keep private.

That concern was cut short, however, when a young woman with rainbow-dyed hair and a smattering of freckles sat down across from me. "You weren't here last night," she noted with an indifferent expression.

I smiled and sat up straighter in my seat. "My husband and I just came in this afternoon. We're on our honeymoon."

She eyed the empty chair beside me and shrugged. "If you say so."

"No, really. He ran into town to get some supplies, but he'll be here soon." I forced another smile, all the while wondering why I cared what this stranger thought of me or my marriage.

She grabbed an apple from the fruit platter in the center of the table and spun it in her hands. "You don't have to prove anything to me. I had a fight with my boyfriend and decided to stay here until he comes back to his senses. Name's Blaire, if that matters to you."

"Angie," I answered with an awkward wiggle of my fingers. "Nice to meet you."

"Yeah, sure. Whatever." Blaire brought the apple close to her face and stared at it for a few moments before returning it to the platter.

An elderly couple shuffled into the dining room

just seconds before the grandfather clock in the hallway chimed eight.

"Good evening!" the man crowed, pulling out a chair for his partner. They were both dressed in khaki shorts and Hawaiian shirts, very obvious tourists. Probably retirees too.

"Isn't it a beautiful evening?" the woman asked Blaire, who simply shrugged and turned away.

"It's lovely," I chimed in, feeing bad about how rude the rainbow-haired twentysomething was being, even though I wasn't responsible for her. "Tomorrow, I'll have to watch the sunset in the garden before dinner. I bet it looks absolutely stunning above all those gorgeous flowers."

All eyes zoomed to me. The man's jaw fell open, and the woman shook her head before folding her hands in her lap.

"Sorry, I didn't mean to speak out of turn. My name's Angie," I said, trying to salvage the interaction.

"Her *husband* and her are here honeymooning," Blaire supplied, making sure to add air quotes around the word *husband*.

The woman curled her lip before offering the fakest smile I'd ever seen in my life. "Well, it's nice to meet you, Angie. Although I suspect you're the reason we were denied our favorite suite despite being very loyal customers to this here estab-lishment."

Heat rushed to my cheeks and I turned my eyes to the table in front of me. "Sorry about that," I murmured.

"I'm sure you wouldn't have stolen our room if you'd known, honey. All is fine." She offered me a saccharine expression that made me feel sick to my stomach.

Thankfully, Madame Blue and Billy chose that precise moment to enter the dining room, each carrying a large silver platter piled with food.

"Salisbury steak," the old woman announced, plunking her tray down before the lone male at the table.

"Mashed potatoes." Billy added his tray to the center of the table, then both returned to the kitchen. When they came back, they delivered a bowl of buttered peas and freshly baked sourdough bread.

"It smells so good," I gushed, sucking in a deep lungful of the savory scents as I reached for the dish nearest to me.

"No, honey. It should be age before beauty," the tourist woman said, shooting daggers my way.

I shrank back from the platter and waited for the

others to serve themselves before I risked a second attempt. Tomorrow Charles and I would definitely be grabbing all our meals at a restaurant. Somehow the guests here were even worse than the staff, but I wouldn't let them spoil my honeymoon.

Improvise, adapt, and overcome. That's what my dad would say if he were here.

Plus this place was special to my parents, and I wanted to experience firsthand all the good memories they'd carried with them over the years. It would be rude to turn our noses up at their gift and book a chain hotel for the week when this place was already paid for. Besides, our room was to die for. I couldn't blame my cruel dining companion for being upset over losing it, but then again, she shouldn't be blaming *me* either.

Once I'd piled my plate with food, Bill and Madame Blue each took a seat at the heads of the table.

"Where's your fella?" our cook asked several notches too loud on the volume scale.

"He just ran into town for a couple supplies. He'll be back soon," I answered meekly. Thanks to the onslaught of sarcasm and snide remarks from the other guests, I was no longer feeling in the mood for conversation of any sort.

She frowned at the bowl of peas. "Supper is at eight p.m. sharp. Didn't you tell them, Billy?"

"Yes, that's the first thing I told them," he said, bobbing his head. "I can share the rules, but I can't force anyone to follow them."

She huffed but said nothing more as she served herself scant portions from each dish.

I made it my mission to finish my food at record speed, hardly taking the time to appreciate the perfect creamy consistency of the mashed potatoes as I shoved them down my gullet and swallowed hard. If Charles wasn't back soon, he'd miss out entirely, but I didn't think he'd mind when I filled him in on what I'd experienced.

I'd finished eating everything except for my last few bites of steak when the lights flickered out, ensconcing the room in darkness.

"Oopsie daisy!" Madame Blue shouted, the same way she shouted everything else. "Billy, grab the candles while I go futz with the fuse box!"

Her cries were met with silence. The older tourist couple seemed to whisper amongst themselves, but I couldn't make out what they were saying.

"Billy?" Blue shouted again. "Billy? Oh for Pete's sake, I'll get the candles myself." Her chair noisily slid out from the table as she continued to grumble to herself. "Honestly, what's the point of hiring paid help if they're never around when you need help?"

I grabbed my phone from my pocket and turned on the flashlight. Unfortunately, I'd had it angled too high and the light shined directly into Blaire's eyes across the table.

"Ahh, are you trying to blind me or what?" she groused, moving her hands in front of her face.

"Sorry, gotta go," I murmured, quickly making tracks back to the staircase. They didn't need me to fix the lighting, but if Charlene woke up to a dark, empty room, she'd be terrified.

I had to get to her—and fast. I just hoped Charles would be back with the two of us soon. I needed his strength and positive outlook now more than ever.

6

returned to a dark room and sleeping kitten. Of course it took a bit of searching with the flashlight on my phone before I finally spotted her snuggled beneath one of the pillows near the headboard of the bed.

Seeing as she was still sound asleep and Charles had yet to return, I spent some time reading a new book from my favorite series on my phone. I managed to squeeze in three full chapters before my husband returned with the supplies.

"Why are all the lights out?" he asked upon entering, his arms encumbered by two large paper grocery bags.

I closed my e-reading app and shone my phone's light toward him in the doorway. "Good question. It went out during dinner. That was more than half an hour ago."

"How hard is it to flip a switch in the fuse box?" he grumbled as he made his way over to me. "Maybe I should go offer to help."

"I wouldn't," I said before filling him in on the details of the quickie dinner party.

"It sounds like each person we meet is worse than the last," he remarked, setting the bags on the loveseat by the fireplace. "I think I met Blaire, assuming she was the rainbow-haired girl slinking around downstairs. I almost ran straight into her when I came through the front door."

"Yup, that would be her. I wonder what she was doing downstairs while all the lights are out, though."

"No idea. She said something about me being the prodigal husband and laughed before turning around and going the opposite direction."

Well, at least now she knew he was real. Not that it mattered—or at least it shouldn't have.

"Is Charlene up?" Charles added while crinkling the bags, presumably as he searched through them.

I shook my head, then realizing he couldn't see me at present, added, "Nope. Not yet."

"Well, let me see if I can start a fire to give us a little more light." More crinkling noises followed.

I came over holding up the flashlight to help light the area while he examined the hearth and surrounding area.

He bent down and poked at the wood waiting in the fireplace. "Darn, these logs are fake. I think it's just meant to be decorative."

I sighed at this. "Welp, no fire for us. Seems about right, given how everything else has been since we arrived."

"It's okay. I can keep you warm," he growled flirtatiously. He grabbed me in his arms and settled for a not-quite-so-quick kiss.

"Stop it. We have a baby in the room with us, remember?"

"Oh, yeah. We really need to make quick work of finding her mother, huh? Should we wake her up to feed her?"

I nodded, still wrapped in my husband's embrace. "Probably a good call. Let's take her and the supplies outside. At least there we have the moonlight."

"And we can kill two birds with one stone by searching for her mother while we're out there," he added before pressing his lips to my forehead and then letting me go.

I scowled at him, illuminated by the bright light

of my phone screen. "Charles, you know I hate that expression."

"Oops. I forgot." His features pinched in apology. "Guess it totally changes meaning when the birds are friends of yours."

"It's okay." I kept the flashlight trained on him as he grabbed a few supplies and then held them up with a grin.

"Ready when you are," he said a few seconds later.

I padded over to the bed and tried implementing the same gradual awakening from before, but Charlene was out—just like all the lights. I frowned. "Maybe we should take her to the vet to get looked over. I'm really starting to worry about her."

"Everything will be closed up for the night by now, but let's get some food in her and see if she perks up. If not, we can go first thing in the morning," Charles said from where he waited near the door.

"Good idea." I leaned down over the bed. "I'm going to pick you up now," I whispered, then did just that.

Charlene sighed and stretched, offering proof of life, but she still didn't wake up.

"Let's go," I said, balancing the kitten and my

phone light as best I could while we made our way to the garden.

Sure enough, it was easier to see outside, but I still needed my light to avoid trampling any of the beautiful flowerbeds by accident. We wove along the trails until we reached the bricked property line, close to the spot where Charles had first discovered the kitten.

"If her mother is going to come back searching for her, she'll check here first," I reasoned, shutting off my flashlight and settling myself on the lawn with my legs crossed beneath me.

"Do you think she'll be back?" Charles whispered, almost as if he were afraid to speak the words.

I placed a hand on Charlene's back to make sure she was still sleeping and breathing both. When I was certain she hadn't stirred, I whispered back in answer to my husband's question. "It's not looking good," I admitted with a soft sigh. "But we'll keep trying. Charlene says she's been gone a long time, but that could mean anything. It may have only been a couple hours when we found her for all we know."

"She's very weak for having only been on her own for a little while," he pointed out with a sad expression.

"Well, all we can do is try our hardest and hope

for the best," I answered while thoughtfully stroking the smooth black fur.

"I'm going to get her dinner together," he said after we both sat in silence for a few minutes. "I wasn't sure how old she is and what she can handle. Plus I remember hearing cats shouldn't have cow's milk. Something about them being lactose intolerant. But I found special cat milk and some soft food made specifically for kittens." He grabbed a pair of small stainless steel bowls and poured the specialized milk into one. "It took a while to find a pet store that was still open, but I managed to sneak into one a few minutes before closing."

"I'm sure Charlene will appreciate it. She's gotta be starving."

Charles pulled the metal ring on the kitten food can next.

"What's that smell?" the kitten mewled from my lap almost immediately.

I chuckled. All cats are the same, whether young or old, pet or stray. "We have some dinner for you," I enthused, setting her on the ground in front of the two bowls just as Charles finished plopping the kitten pate into the second dish.

She went straight for the tuna-flavored mush,

making yummy noises as she snarfed it down as quickly as her tiny mouth would allow.

"Would you look at that?" Charles remarked, his green eyes fixing on the baby lovingly. "Looks like I did good."

"You did great," I said, reaching over to rub him on the shoulder. Charles and I both thought it would be best to wait a couple years before starting a family, but at least now I saw he would make a truly fantastic dad when the time came. Maybe that would be sooner rather than later, after all.

harlene finished half of her wet food before moving on to the milk, which she proceeded to lap up just as enthusiastically. Her ability to eat solid foods was encouraging. Perhaps she wasn't as young as we'd initially feared. But the fact that such a tiny thing was eating so much at one go suggested she'd been on her own for far too long. It's a good thing Charles and I found her before some predator had.

"You stay here," I told my husband, carefully pushing myself to my feet. "I'm going to search for Charlene's mother."

I flipped my phone light back on and started my hunt. I really needed to get more information from the kitten about what her mother looked like, but I also didn't want to upset the frightened little thing any more than I had to. That meant right now I was simply looking for a cat—any cat.

"Here, kitty, kitty!" I called softly, unsure whether this strategy would even work. But what choice did I have?

I moved closer to the house, checking for any hidey holes that might attract an animal in search of shelter. "Hello?" I called.

No one answered. Of course no one did.

I moved around the house to the backyard. The gardens back here weren't as neatly kept as those out front, but still very impressive all the same. I stopped to admire a small vegetable patch and wondered if this was where supper's buttered peas had originated.

After only a very brief pause, I carried forward, making clicking noises that I hoped would entice any cat who might be listening.

Zip! A fast flash of movement on the periphery caught my eye, and I spun around. Whatever I'd noticed had already disappeared from view, however.

"Hello?" I called, voice shaking. Was this the missing mother cat or a roaming murderer? I shuddered again and vowed to stop watching so many true crime documentaries in the future.

Swallowing down that sudden lump of fear, I

moved decisively in the direction of the movement. And my senses screamed at me—specifically my sense of smell.

"What is that?" I groaned, waving a hand before my face to help dissipate the awful aroma. With one hand pinching my nose, I used the other to wave my light around until it landed on a huge leafy green plant. Yup, that was definitely the source of the smell. *Gross.*

I snapped a quick photo before turning tail and moving as fast as I could in the other direction.

When I returned to Charles and Charlene, I found that both bowls of food had been licked completely clean. Now a full-bellied fur baby was resting on my husband's lap and purring so loud I could hear it from several paces away.

"Any sign of her?" he asked hopefully, but I just shook my head.

Charlene stopped purring. "Why hasn't my mommy come back?" she demanded, her eyes roving across the garden. Unlike us she could see perfectly in the night. Her hearing beat ours too, which Octo-Cat had reminded me several times over the years—along with every other way cats are superior to humans.

"We haven't found her yet, but we aren't giving

up," I assured the little one, taking a seat beside her and Charles. "Can you maybe tell us a bit more about her?"

Charlene closed her eyes and purred softly as she called upon the memories of her mother. "She is the nicest mommy ever with very soft fur for cuddling and very sharp teeth and claws for hunting. I want to be just like her when I grow up!"

"What does she look like?" I prompted gently.

The kitten closed her eyes again, whiskers twitching as she thought. "She's black with brown spots, long whiskers, and a very pink tongue."

I got out my phone again and did a quick web search. "Kind of like this?" I asked, showing her a photo of a tortoiseshell cat.

"That's not my mommy," Charlene cried, offended for a moment before softening in defeat. "But I guess she looks a little like that."

"Okay, I'm going to show you some more photos, and you can let me know if any of them are your mommy." I typed in *animal rescues near me* and then began scrolling through the photos of adoptable cats, pausing over any mostly black cats to share the photos with Charlene.

But none were a match for the missing mama cat.

"My eyes hurt," the kitten squeaked, squinting

them tight. All that blue light must have been bad for her. Oops. So much to learn about babies before I had any of my own.

"We'll stop for tonight," I said tenderly, "but we'll start looking again first thing tomorrow morning."

"You promise?" she asked meekly, her ears falling flat against her head.

"Of course, I promise." I scratched gently at her tiny forehead to reassure her. "Are you okay spending the night inside our room with us?"

Her ears lifted, but she still appeared to be on high alert, ready to run off at any moment. "I think so. You promise not to eat me, right?"

I laughed. "Yes, I promise that too."

"And he won't either?" she asked, turning to look up at Charles with sudden suspicion.

"Neither of us eat cats," I assured her very firmly. "You're safe with us."

As we headed back toward the house, the lights finally flickered on.

"About time," Charles remarked as he concealed Charlene in his large hands.

I glanced up at the house and saw a dark figure backlit in one of the bedroom windows upstairs. It looked like it could be ours, but surely I just had my wires crossed. I wasn't the best with directions, even when I had a GPS to help me. And from my count, there were at least eight bedrooms on the second story, which meant the figure was more than likely occupying one that wasn't ours.

Still, the eerie sight sent a chill straight through me. I glanced toward Charles, but he just kept striding swiftly ahead, completely unaware.

When I looked up at the window again, the figure had vanished, leaving me to wonder if my mind was simply playing tricks on me.

"Careful," Charles warned, his eyes staring straight down as he held the door open for me. "There's mud everywhere."

Sure enough, fresh, wet mud had been tromped across the downstairs. It was too messy to discern clear footprints, but that was clearly the source.

I sucked air in through my teeth. "Oh, Madame Blue is not going to be happy about that."

"Well, just as long as she doesn't blame us," Charles grumbled.

I made extra sure to avoid the filthy rug at the base of the stairs so there would be no question that another guest was responsible for the mess.

But suddenly I found myself feeling a bit guilty about keeping a secret pet on the premises. Madame Blue had been very clear about the rules, and she obviously had a lot to worry about, given her constant grumblings. I didn't want to contribute to her problems, but the lost kitten needed help and I refused to turn my back on that.

I guess it wouldn't be a problem as long as we didn't get caught... At least that's what I told myself as we tucked in for the night.

8

"*AAAAAAAH!*" a rough scream jolted me from sleep the next morning.

The kitten beside me jumped at least two feet straight into the air and hissed as I grabbed my robe from the love seat near the non-functioning fireplace and ran out into the hall to see what had happened.

"Is everything okay?" I asked a confused-looking Blaire, who hadn't bothered to cover up before stepping into the hall. She rubbed at her eyes and then pointed to the narrow staircase where my husband crouched midway down the steps. No, he wasn't crouched. He'd *fallen* partway through. Splintered wood shot up in jagged spikes all around him. I couldn't see his face, but I assumed he wore an expression of great pain.

"Charles!" I shouted, rushing forward to the edge of the broken staircase. "What happened?"

He grunted and attempted to turn toward me, but shifting his weight caused him to fall a few inches farther into the hole. He let out a long groan before saying, "I was going to surprise you. With biscuits and gravy for breakfast at sunrise," he murmured with the back of his head facing me.

"We have to get you out of there!" I shouted, spinning around in search of someone other than Blaire, who clearly didn't have the strength—or the inclination—to assist us. "Billy? Madame Blue? Can someone please help?"

"Now what's all this fuss about so early in the morning?" the man from the tourist couple asked, pulling open his bedroom door and breezing down the hallway in our direction.

"My husband!" I cried, pointing frantically. "He fell through the stairs and needs help getting out!"

He turned to look and actually had the audacity to chuckle. "You're right. That's quite the pickle he's gotten himself into." He raised his voice to call to Charles. "Hold your horses, son. I'll grab Bill and be right down to help you out."

"This is not how I wanted to start my day." The man's wife appeared wearing another Hawaiian shirt and khakis get-up along with a look of consternation. "Nothing like this ever happened during our other stays."

I bit my tongue to avoid saying something I'd regret.

"So cringe," Blaire said with a laugh before returning to her room. She reappeared a few seconds later holding her phone out before her. "I know just the sound to use with this video, too," she said, leaving no doubt that she was turning my husband's misfortune into a TikTok meme.

"Charles, are you hurt?" I called, choosing to ignore the other guests and focus on what was really important here. "Should I call 9-1-1?"

"More startled than anything," he answered with a sharp grunt. "Knocked the wind right out of me, but nothing's broken."

"Well, let's get you out first, then we can see if we need to visit a doctor." My anxiety had gotten so bad, I wanted to curl into a ball on the floor and start crying—but Charles needed me to be strong, so that's what I tried to do.

"Shoot, what a mess!" Billy said, arriving on the scene with a worn leather tool belt clinched around his waist. "You're going to have to pay for this to be fixed, and it won't be cheap."

"Can you please just get him out of there?" I begged rather than fighting against his ridiculous claim. Right now, he was our best bet for getting Charles back on solid ground.

"We're on it," the tourist man said, appearing at the bottom of the stairs beside Billy. I hadn't spotted a second staircase, but clearly they'd gotten down there somehow, and now they set straight to work on their mission.

Everything seemed to happen in slow motion as Bill and his helper worked to free Charles. For a while I was worried that they'd fall into the hole with him, that the whole house would crumble around us, but eventually they managed to pull him free.

As soon as he was out, I ran down the hall until I found the second set of stairs and bolted down them. When I returned to the base of the broken staircase across the house, I hugged Charles tight. "You had me so worried."

"Angie, I'm fine. Just a couple of Tylenol and a hot bath, and I'll be right as rain." He pulled out of my hug to study me with a piteous expression. "We missed the sunrise, though. And breakfast."

"I'll order some delivery. Let's just get you taken

care of first." I slung an arm around his waist in case he needed the extra support while walking. "Come on, there's a second staircase over this way."

"Not so fast, honey," the tourist woman called from above. "I personally don't feel safe with you two staying on the second floor. What if your oaf of a husband breaks the other stairway? Then we'll all be stuck up here for who knows how long? And, well, it makes much more sense to move the two of you than to have to move us and that other young woman with the crazy hair. Don't you think so, Madame Blue?"

"Better safe than sorry, I suppose," the elderly caretaker shouted back with a scowl, then dropped her voice to grumble to herself. "But either way, the historical society is not going to take kindly to this mishap."

She turned toward me and Charles with a frown. "We do have a room on the first floor. Billy, will you unlock it and help them move their belongings down?"

The tourist woman stood with arms crossed and an enormous smirk on her face. "Thank you for taking such good care of us. And if it's not too much trouble, once you've had a chance to clean out the grand suite, could Fred and I move in? We were originally supposed to have that room anyway, so it works out great for everyone."

"Sure, Madeline. Whatever you want," Madame Blue answered with a sigh before ambling off.

Blaire kept recording the whole scene, but nobody paid her much mind. She did shoot a sympathetic glance my way, though and said, "This really sucks for you."

Honestly, I couldn't have said it better myself, even if I'd tried. And right now I just didn't have the energy.

9

"We could sue them for negligence, seeing as I was injured on their property," Charles told me once we were by ourselves again. The other guests had all gone back to their rooms while Billy worked on seeing to our change in accommodations, and Madame Blue was off doing who knows what.

"But you said you weren't hurt," I reminded him gently. Even if we were in the right, I didn't want to waste any more time with these people when it would be so much easier to just move on with our lives.

"I'm not planning to open a case, but it's just the principle of the matter. Especially if they're going to ask for the cost of repairs. That's definitely not legal." Charles pulled out his phone and opened the search window, ready to jump into lawyer mode despite his claims.

I pushed his hand down and shook my head. "They really seem to be in dire financial straits. I wonder what else isn't to code. Charles, that was really scary. I'm not sure if I feel safe staying here for another night. Let's focus on that rather than researching legal action you don't plan to take."

He nodded and tucked his phone back into his jeans pocket. "I understand, Angie. We can't leave, though. Not until we find Charlene's mother."

"Shoot, Charlene!" I cried. Even if Billy and Madame Blue were in the wrong when it came to Charles's accident, we were in the wrong too by willfully disregarding their rules.

"I have to get back up there and hide her before Billy moves all our things and locks us out. I'll meet you at the new room as soon as I have her, okay?"

Charles gave me a peck on the cheek. "I'll wait here and see about getting some breakfast ordered."

"Love you," I called before heading back up the second, unbroken staircase.

When I reached the room, Billy was already there gathering our things for relocation. The tourist woman—Madeline, apparently—was also there, observing the fireplace. "It won't be any problem to get this lit for us tonight, would it?" she said to the porter, not really making it a question.

"Um, excuse me," I barked, not even trying to be polite with them anymore. "Until we're moved, this room still belongs to me and my husband, and we'd appreciate some privacy." I returned the same daggers Madeline had thrown at me over dinner last night.

She narrowed her eyes before switching to a tight-lipped smile. "Whatever you say, honey. It will be ours soon enough." Thankfully, she saw herself out after having stated her piece.

Once she was gone, I stepped into the bathroom where Bill was haphazardly tossing our toiletries into a plastic grocery bag. "Um, Bill, we appreciate your help, but can I please pack up my own belongings? I don't really like the idea of a stranger handling my toothbrush... or my underwear."

"The lady of the house wants it all moved ASAP," he explained, continuing his work undeterred. "Between you and me, she doesn't want to deal with the Mackenzies any more than you do."

"I understand that, but could you just wait out in the hall for a few minutes? I promise I'll get it done quick."

He nodded, handed me the plastic bag, and left, clicking the door shut behind him.

"Charlene?" I whisper-yelled once I knew for sure we were alone.

A moment later, she pushed her little black head out from beneath my pillow. Oh, thank goodness!

"I don't like it here," she growled, surprising me with her deep rumble. "Too many scary people."

I nodded in understanding. Frankly, I found them a bit scary too. "Charles and I will keep you safe until you're back with your mother. You have my word, Charlene. We won't let anything bad happen to you."

"I thought I heard my mommy calling to me last night, but it was just a dream." This sweet kitten kept breaking my heart.

"Dreams do come true," I offered, running my hands over her fur. "But right now we have to get you out of here. They're making us switch rooms, but after that, we'll head back outside to look around, okay?"

She responded by purring and asking to be picked up.

"Perfect. Let's go." I quickly shoved all our loose belongings—along with Billy's plastic bag—into one of Charles's duffle bags, then grabbed a spare sweater to wrap the kitten in while I moved her downstairs.

"Ready for you now. Thank you, Bill," I said as I left the dream room behind. With how terrible everyone had been since we'd arrived, Bill was the only one to show even the slightest glimpse of compassion—be it exceptionally brief. "We appreciate your help."

"Your new room is just off the kitchen. It isn't much. We usually only book it if all the rooms are already spoken for, which hasn't happened in a really long time. But you can easily sneak anything you need from the fridge, so there's that," he offered apologetically. "I'll meet you in the kitchen. Just give me two shakes of a lamb's tail."

"Thank you," I said again before heading back down the long hall and toward the second staircase. As I passed, Madeline and Fred Mackenzie watched me from their doorway with matching expressions of glee. I hated that they were getting what they wanted after such gruesome behavior, but there wasn't a thing I could do about it.

"They're putting us by the kitchen," I told Charles when I joined back up with him, motioning toward the bundle that concealed Charlene with my chin.

"Excellent," he answered calmly. "I am more than ready for those Tylenol. And that bath."

"No bathtub in your new room," Billy said, coming up behind us with one duffle balanced on the suitcase and the other slung over his shoulder. "No bathroom at all, actually. You'll have to use the communal on the first floor. Thankfully, we added a shower stall to it a few years back for just such emergencies."

That was when I finally lost it. My husband had been grievously injured and all he wanted was a hot bath. Why were they making that impossible for us in a literal mansion with multiple accommodations?

"Surely, you see how ridiculous this is?" I hissed, no longer playing nice. "Charles isn't a liability, he's a victim. And my parents paid for your best room, thinking they were reserving the full property, but now you're shoving us into your smallest room because of some other guest's unfounded complaint?"

Billy shrugged, unmoved and apparently unsurprised by my outburst. "If it upsets you, give us a bad review. It's no skin off my back. It's only Madame Blue you'll be hurting, since she's the owner and all."

"You said we'd have to pay for the damages," I reminded him, the rage continuing to build.

He clicked his tongue in disagreement. "I said that to keep my job. I knew that old biddy would be listening."

"If you hate her so much, why do you work here?"

"Hard to beat a job that includes room and board in this economy. Now, after you." He pushed the door open to reveal a room that barely contained the lone queen-sized bed. A tall dresser stood in the corner, and a folding TV tray had been topped with a lamp and doily as some kind of makeshift nightstand. Otherwise, that was it.

"You're kidding me. This is barely more than a closet!" I protested as Bill set our bags by the dresser, taking up almost half of the unoccupied floor space.

"At least the garden is nice," Charles said once the porter had left us to our own devices.

"Most of it, anyway," I shot back, remembering the foul patch of greenery I'd stumbled upon the night before. "Oh, I didn't show you what I found last night." I set Charlene on the new bed, then pulled out my phone and thumbed through the camera roll.

"Here," I said, shoving the screen toward him. "I found this around the back when I was searching for Charlene's mother last night. It smelled terrible."

His face lit with amusement. "Like a skunk?"

"Yeah, actually. How did you—?"

"That's skunk cabbage. Doesn't make much sense to have it in a garden that's as well maintained as this one. Then again, given the condition of the stairs, maybe the garden isn't as well maintained as we once thought."

"What is going on with this place? It's nothing like my mom described, and I doubt it's anything like she remembers. Almost as if everything that could go wrong has."

"Shhh, you'll jinx it," Charles said with a playful wink. Well, at least I had the best possible company for my week in hell.

10

fed the kitten inside our downsized room while Charles grabbed a quick shower in the first-floor communal bathroom. When he returned, claiming to feel much better, we both got dressed so we could head outside to further investigate the gardens.

"I couldn't find a place that delivers this far out," I revealed as Charles pulled on his shoes. "So let's eat some of the snacks you brought last night and then we can go to town for an early lunch after we've spent a few hours searching."

"Fair enough. I'll grab the snacks," he offered without complaint.

"I'll grab Charlene." She'd wasted no time in sandwiching herself between the mattress and pillow of the new bed.

After a brisk walk across the property, Charles and I settled ourselves at an iron bistro table that stood flanked by two ornate chairs.

"Doritos and beef jerky for breakfast," I quipped, eagerly digging into the snack food. "Living the high life."

"Only the best for my wifey," Charles teased, crunching into a bright orange tortilla chip. "And if you're really good, I'll share my Oreos with you."

"Can't refuse an offer like that," I joked right back.

The two us ate in companionable silence as the three of us kept our eyes and ears peeled for Charlene's missing mother.

"Do you hear that?" I asked after a short while had passed.

Charles straightened in his seat. "What? A cat?"

I strained to hear more clearly but was met with little more than a stream of hushed whispers from across the garden. "I'm not sure. There's multiple voices. They're quiet, though. I can't hear what they're saying."

"Well, let's go find out." Charles stood and brushed his hands together to rid them of the flavor dust.

I sucked each of my fingers clean, then we headed back toward the yellow roses that had so enchanted me the previous afternoon.

"Do you hear them? The voices?" I asked, glancing around but still not finding the speakers.

He shook his head. "Must be an animal. You know I'm useless when it comes to that."

"You're not useless," I insisted before glancing to the kitten in my arms for aid. "Do you hear anyone, Charlene?"

"No, sorry," she mewed sadly. Huh, that was weird.

"Hello?" I called hesitantly as we continued toward the yellow roses.

Finally the words started to make sense. "And that's another thing. I know the lights went out, but if they couldn't see, they should have stayed put. Someone trampled the flower beds out back. They almost stomped right on the queen. The queen!"

"Humans, they're the worst. Almost as bad as that pesky skunk," a second mystery speaker agreed.

"Hear, hear!" several voices chimed at once.

"Hello?" I tried again. "Who's there?"

"What are those two humans doing so close to our hive? Should we sting them?" one of the soft voices ground out.

"Please don't sting me," I cried, now understanding without a doubt whose conversation I was overhearing. "I'm a friend to all creatures. Including bees."

"Is she talking to us? No human has ever done that before." A confused buzzing followed.

I lifted Charlene closer to my face and asked. "Are you sure you can't hear anyone?"

"Nope," the little kitten confirmed. Usually animals had no problem understanding each other, but then again, I'd never spoken with insects before. I'd never heard them until now. I swear, this honeymoon of ours just kept getting stranger and stranger.

With my companions unable to offer assistance, I pressed forward all on my own. "Hello, bees. I'm talking to you. I'm sorry about the trampled flowers and that someone almost hurt your queen. I can help, if you'll talk to me."

I waited as the voices whispered amongst themselves, clearly not wanting to be overheard until they reached some kind of unanimous decision about me.

Finally, one plump bee flew out to greet me face to face. "Greetings, human. I am Aldrin and this is Lightyear." He waited as a second buzzing insect joined us.

"Hello. I'm Angie." I stayed stock still, but Charles jumped behind me.

"Oh boy. More bees. I'm just going to go grab my EpiPen, just in case. I'll take Charlene too." As soon as I transferred the kitten to his arms, my husband took off like a shot.

"You do not fear us, human," Aldrin noted, bobbing in the air.

"Angie," I reminded him with a gentle voice. "Call me Angie."

"Apologies. We have not spoken to any human before. Are you the one who lives in the house?" I couldn't tell whether this came from Aldrin or Lightyear. I wasn't sure that it mattered, since the bees all seemed to act and think as one.

"No, I'm just here on vacation." I chose not to point out that Madame Blue and I looked nothing alike, seeing as she was several decades older, much shorter, and much louder as a general rule. I'd guess that all humans looked the same to bees, the way all bees tended to look the same to humans.

The two bees buzzed back and forth to each other, communicating with a series of movements rather than words. When at last they seemed to agree, they spoke to me again. "Then would you share our complaints with the human who does?"

"I can try," I answered truthfully. I could barely share my own complaints with Madame Blue and Billy, and I was a paying guest. I didn't think they'd agree to do anything to help the bees, but I would at least try.

"Good enough for us," Lightyear decided, and both bees bounced up and down.

Aldrin was the one who delivered their list of grievances. "Our gardens used to flourish, giving us an abundance of delicious honey, but lately the landscape is looking bleak. Some of our favorite flowers are disappearing, only to be replaced with poor substitutes."

"The skunk cabbage," I said, thinking back to last night plus Charles's later identification of the plant.

Both bees zigzagged in a frenzy before calming down enough to speak again. "Skunks are natural enemies of bees. Someone is attempting to threaten us, and we do not take kindly to it. Our honey is also being over-harvested, and it's not leaving enough to nourish our hive. We are happy for humans enjoy the fruits of our labor in moderation, but now our sustenance is being stolen right from under us. We work hard and yet our bellies remain empty into the next day."

"I'm really sorry. That sounds horrible." I sympathized with them even though I had little basis for understanding the secret lives of bees.

"It is quite horrible," they said in unison, moving in a synchronized aerial dance.

"I will see what I can do for you," I assured them. Maybe if I asked some questions about the skunk cabbage I'd found and where I could buy some local honey, Madame Blue would inadvertently open up to me.

"That is all we ask," one of the bees said before both flitted back to the hive somewhere out of sight.

Charles and I had come to this old stone mansion nearly a thousand miles away from home to get away from it all. Yet somehow we found ourselves plagued by mystery after mystery. If it weren't for one very sweet kitten needing our help, we would already be gone. But since we were stuck for the time being, we might as well try to solve a couple of these mysteries and hopefully leave the place better than we found it.

11

Once the bees left me, I decided to wander the property line in hopes of finding Charlene's mother. The entire yard was marked with a red brick fence running around the perimeter, but there was plenty of nature on the other side of the fence, too. Maybe we should expand our search to the neighboring properties as well. I'd ask Charles for his thoughts on the matter when he returned with his EpiPen.

Halfway through my second circle around the garden, Blaire barged out through the front door, shouting into her phone. The sunlight reflected beautifully off her multi-hued hair, making me wonder if I could pull off such a bold look myself.

I tried not to listen to her conversation as I quietly

continued my search, but Blaire's voice carried across the open space.

"Maybe I don't want to come home! Did you ever think about that?" she practically snarled while I busied myself inspecting the hydrangeas.

A few moments later, she laughed bitterly. "You really think that, huh? Do not—I repeat, *do not*—come here. I don't want to see you right now, Dylan, and at this rate, I'm not sure I ever want to see your stupid face again!"

I stole a glance at Blaire and found her freckled face now covered with red splotches, too. The poor thing. She was so young to have such intense domestic troubles. Should I offer to help somehow?

She caught me staring and scowled my way.

I quickly averted my gaze.

"I've gotta go," she said much more quietly to the person on the other end of the call—presumably a boyfriend named Dylan. "There's some nosy lady listening in. And besides, I have nothing to say to you anyway."

She ended the call and then let out a primal scream before rounding on me. "Enjoying your daily dose of *schadenfreude*?" she yelled before marching straight back inside and slamming the door behind her.

Well, at least it seemed like Blaire could take care of herself, even if she was no great fan of mine. Hopefully, she knew not to go back to a boyfriend who wasn't treating her right.

One day she would find her Charles.

I took a moment to luxuriate in the love I had for my new husband, only to realize I hadn't seen him for quite a while. He'd left when I was speaking with the bees, promising to be right back after he'd grabbed his EpiPen. He definitely should have returned by now.

Unless something bad happened?

Oh my gosh, it was the broken staircase all over again. Generally, I wasn't a very superstitious person, but we were definitely living according to Murphy's Law since arriving in Virginia. Everything that could go wrong was—and then some.

I quickened my pace, suddenly desperate to find Charles. I ran to the base of the broken staircase first but couldn't see him there. I did, however, hear a faint pounding from the back of the house, so I ran that way next.

"Charles?" I called, tracing my way through the kitchen toward our new bedroom.

"Angie? Is that you? I'm locked in!" he called glumly through the door.

"Locked in? What happened?" I grabbed the doorknob and attempted to turn it, but it was definitely stuck. *Ugh!*

"I don't know," my husband's tired, muffled voice answered. "It took me a couple minutes to find my EpiPen since our stuff was all mixed up from changing rooms. By the time I found it and went to leave, the door wouldn't budge. I've been calling for help a while now, but nobody's answered."

I knew that Blaire had been occupied by her phone call, but where was everyone else? Why wasn't anyone helping? Well, at least I was here now—for all the good that did.

"I can't get it to open, either. I'm going to find help!" I shouted, hating to leave him there.

Billy had been more or less gracious about helping us earlier, but what would he think now that we had a second crisis on our hands within the span of just a couple short hours? If he'd heard Charles calling, he'd chosen to ignore him.

I searched the house for any sign of life—I even attempted knocking on the guest rooms upstairs, but nobody answered my cries for help, even though I swore I could hear Blaire moving about in her room, not that she'd be able to offer much help anyway.

Having exhausted my options inside, I swung back by our room to tell Charles I was still searching for someone to open the door, then stormed outside quickly reaching my rope's end. I remembered seeing an old toolshed on the far edge of the property; maybe I could find something to help me take the door off its hinges. Right now that seemed like the best option, because nobody else was here and I certainly didn't trust myself to pick a lock.

I'd stalked halfway to the shed when the same old pickup truck we'd parked beside upon arriving rumbled into the driveway. I turned back to the lot and watched as Madame Blue parked and then hopped down, spotting me almost instantly.

"Yes?" she shouted unhappily. "What is it now?"

My cheeks grew hot with embarrassment. "Well, Billy switched our bedroom to the one downstairs, and now the door won't open. My husband is stuck inside."

"Stuck? Oh, for crying out loud. If it's not one thing, it's the other. Can't even leave for one hour to run an errand in town. Things like this are exactly why the bank denied my loan. They don't think the place is worth saving, and sad to say I'm starting to agree." She shook her head and fumbled with her keys.

I could see she was in no mood to be bothered, but I also needed her help to free Charles, leaving me no choice but to press her further. "I'm really sorry to bother you with this. It's just that he's locked in there with no food and no bathroom."

"Yeah, yeah, I'm coming," she groused, pulling her purse strap high over her shoulder as she marched past me and into the house.

When she tried the doorknob and found that it was, indeed, stuck, she returned to the kitchen to grab a step stool. After setting it in front of the door, she climbed on top, then swiped her hand over the doorframe and pulled down an old brass key, stuck it in the knob, and pushed the door open.

"Now, if you don't mind, I'm behind on preparing the day's lunch," she huffed, leaving me and Charles to stare at each other with bemused expressions.

"I didn't know there was a key," I told him with a wince before falling into his arms to offer a giant hug.

He stroked my hair to soothe me, even though he was the one whose safety had once again been compromised. "Somebody must have locked me in, but why?"

"That, my dear, is a very good question."

He was right. Somebody was definitely out to get him, and I needed to discover who before anything else bad transpired.

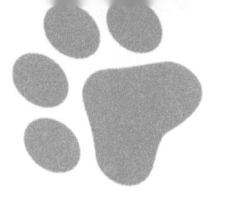

12

Charles's stomach growled as we were resting on the bed together.

"I guess assorted snack food doesn't exactly make the best breakfast, especially since you missed dinner last night," I told him while Charlene snoozed tucked into his side.

"Yeah, but no one delivers out here, and we can't exactly leave Charlene." He paused to run his hand over the kitten a few times before turning his attention back to me. "Madame Blue mentioned making lunch, right? Maybe we should just brave another awkward meal with the others. Once we find Charlene's mother, we can go into town for a massive nine-course meal."

"And we could book a new place to stay while

we're there," I added with a sigh, rolling over onto my side to face him. "But are you sure about waiting to leave?"

"What better option do we have? We can't leave this baby on her own, and we can't exactly trust anyone else here with her."

"We could take her with us to the new hotel," I suggested, already knowing that wasn't really an option.

Charles's green eyes bored into me. "But then we'd have no reason to come back to the property. You and I both know Madame Blue would kick us out in a heartbeat."

"True." I picked at the skin on my elbow, a nasty nervous habit. "I'm just worried something else bad will happen."

He shook his head, also shaking off my concern. "We'll be fine."

"I know I will be, but what about you?"

"I'll be fine too," he assured me despite loads of evidence to the contrary, but he had a smile on his face again. "Now let's go eat before my stomach starts making some truly terrifying noises."

I still felt unsure about joining the others but had to admit we were in a pretty tight spot. Reluctantly, I joined Charles, making sure to swipe the key from the top of the doorframe so nobody else had access to it while we were staying inside. We found Madame Blue, Billy, and the Mackenzie couple eating pastrami sandwiches and what appeared to be potato salad.

"No Blaire today?" I asked casually as Charles and I took our seats.

"She does intermittent fasting. Some trendy Zoomer thing," Madeline Mackenzie explained with a huge grin pointed my way. She seemed to be in a far better mood now that she had the room she wanted. Good riddance.

Charles pulled the platter of sandwiches across the table and helped himself to two on rye, leaving the sourdough for me.

I spooned big heaps of the salad onto each of our plates while he polished off the first triangle of his first sandwich. Something green mixed into the creamy potatoes caught my eye, causing me to take a closer look at the lump on my plate. Yup, capers.

That was one food I truly despised, and there would be no eating around them. The bitter little balls ruined anything they touched—especially my taste buds. *Bleck.*

Charles finished his first sandwich and then dug into his potatoes with great enthusiasm. After taking that first bite, he turned to me and I nodded. A second later, he grabbed my plate and transferred all of my salad over to his. Ah, he knew me so well.

"My cooking not to your liking?" Madame Blue shouted from the other end of the table.

"The sandwiches are delicious," I enthused, pointing toward my plate with one hand and giving a thumbs-up with the other. "I'm just not a fan of capers."

"No class," she muttered to herself, though it was loud enough for everyone to hear.

Mrs. Mackenzie snickered, but then her husband put his hand on her arm and she fell quiet.

Charles seemed to eat even faster after that, wanting to free us quickly while still satisfying his stomach. By the time I finished my sandwich, crusts and all, he was ready to go.

He placed his napkin on his plate and rose to his feet. "Thank you for a delicious meal."

I got up too, then scrambled after him as he strode swiftly toward our room, which was now very close to the dining area.

At the door, Charles's stomach gurgled loudly.

"Didn't you get enough to eat?" I teased.

He grimaced and placed a hand to his belly. "Just need to make a quick trip to the bathroom. I'll be back with you soon." He bent to offer me a kiss, but then quickly changed his mind and took off power-walking in the direction of the communal restroom.

I shrugged and let myself into the room to check on Charlene.

She woke up when I joined her on the bed. "Where's your mate?" she asked, searching the small room for Charles.

"He'll be back soon. How are you feeling?"

"Still sad about Mommy, but I'm not so sleepy anymore." She licked her paw and ran it over her head.

"That's good!" I enthused as the kitten settled herself on my lap.

"Yeah," she said with a heavy sigh, falling over onto her side dramatically in true cat fashion. "But now I'm bored. Would you tell me more of the story of Octavius?"

I chuckled at how wide her bright eyes were when she made this request. "You like that story, huh?"

"Yes, very much." She bobbed her head, already picking up our human gestures after such a short acquaintanceship.

Then I had an idea that I was sure would be a hit. "Want to see a picture of him?"

"Yes!" she squeaked in pleasure, jumping back to

her feet and glancing around the room in confusion. "Where is it?"

"On my phone, one sec." I pulled out my cell phone and flicked through the camera roll, settling on a photo I'd snapped of Octo-Cat and Grizabella on my wedding day, which had somehow turned into their wedding day, too. He looked very handsome in a pink bowtie while she stood at his side with a bow of her own and a fancy lacy veil.

"Wow, I've never seen a cat like that before." Her eyes were trained on the Himalayan, a former show cat and true beauty.

"That's Grizabella. She's his mate," I explained, then pointed to the other side of the photo. "And that's Octavius."

Charlene looked at Octo-Cat briefly before her eyes darted straight back to Grizz. "Does she live with you too?" the kitten wanted to know.

"No," I answered with a sad smile. Of course my cat fell in love with someone on the other side of the country, because life could never be easy. "She lives very far away."

"I bet he misses her when she's not around. Just like I miss my mommy."

"I think you're right about that. Want to see more photos?" I offered, since like every cat owner in the history of existence my camera roll was filled with candid snaps of my furry roommate.

"I want to see all the photos!" she cried, drawing a happy chuckle from me in response.

Charlene was absolutely enamored with my spoiled tabby, asking many questions as we browsed. Finally she squinted her eyes tight and reported that the light was hurting them again. "But we can look at more later, right?"

"We can even call him if you want to meet him. When your eyes are feeling better."

"I would love that very much, but right now I'm feeling sleepy again." She wasted no time curling back into a tight little ball.

"Good night, Charlene," I said, placing a light kiss between her ears.

13

Charles remained in the bathroom for a worryingly long time. At one point, I even got up to check if he'd somehow gotten locked in again, but he assured me—through a tightly shut door—that he was fine and would be out soon.

I tried not to worry, but this was odd behavior for my new husband. Another hour passed before he finally returned to our room, looking absolutely worse for wear.

"I think someone poisoned me," he whispered cautiously.

"Poisoned!" I couldn't help but shout.

"Shhh," he warned, putting a finger to his lips to emphasize the point. "We don't know who's listening. And poison might be too strong a word, but I do suspect there were laxatives mixed in with the pota-toes. You're fine, right?"

"Fit as a fiddle." I spun around with my arms in the air to give him a look at me from all angles, then dropped my arms and frowned. "But do you really think someone slipped you something? That's awful."

He held his stomach and dropped onto the foot of the bed so as not to disturb Charlene who was sleeping near the headboard. "Yeah," he groaned. "Someone's definitely out to get me."

I lay across the middle of the bed between the two of them, turning onto my side to face Charles. A theory was forming in my head.

"Maybe not you specifically," I said, giving that a second to sink in. "If they slipped something into the potatoes, they could have meant to get the both of us. Same with the stairs. They had no way of knowing you'd be first down in the morning. And the room, that could have just as easily been me—or both of us —inside."

Charles thought about this for a moment. "So someone's out to get us. They just keep getting *me* specifically. But why would anyone even want to? We just arrived last night, and nobody knows us here."

"Your guess is as good as mine, and I have no

guesses at all. We do, however, have a fairly limited pool of suspects."

"Madame Blue, Billy, the rainbow-haired girl—"

"Blaire," I provided.

"Right, Blaire, and that older couple who nabbed our room right out from under us." His expression turned sour. "My money's on them."

"The Mackenzies are pretty unpleasant—I'll give you that—but our culprit could really be anyone here. Blaire's made it no secret she doesn't care for me. But it's Billy and Madame Blue who have the best access to everything. Let's assume the stairs were an honest-to-goodness accident. Someone still had to purposely lock you in and lace the potatoes with laxatives."

Charles's eyes lit with understanding. "Madame Blue is the one who prepared the food, which makes her our most likely suspect."

"Maybe, but maybe not. When the lights went out during dinner, she called for Billy to help with the candles, but Billy wasn't there." I just now realized Charles hadn't been there with me during that ill-fated supper. He didn't have all the same firsthand information I did, and I hadn't thought to share these details last night, assuming they were simply minor caveats. Now they could be our biggest clues.

"You think Billy's the one who cut the power?" Charles summed up.

"Honestly, I don't know what to think at this point. The only thing I know for sure is that we're not safe here." A shiver tore through me. I hated to think what might happen next. Poor Charles had already been through the wringer and didn't deserve even a drop of additional trouble.

"But we're stuck until we find Charlene's mother," he said.

We both gazed lovingly at the snoozing kitten.

"One good thing, we have the key to our room now." I pulled it out of my pocket with a grin. "If we spend most of the day in the garden searching for mama cat, we can lock our room whenever we're not in here."

He took the key from me and studied it for a moment before tucking it into his front pocket. "True, and I can go into town around dinner to pick up some takeout and stock up our food supplies again."

I frowned at the thought of him leaving yet again. We weren't supposed to spend even a second apart this week. "I'm sorry our honeymoon has turned into such a downer."

Charles reached for me and pulled me tight to his side. "Angie, dear, we have the rest of our lives together. We'll have a million opportunities to do the big romantic vacation thing some other time."

I forced a smile. I knew he was right, but still, this trip was turning out almost the exact opposite of what I'd anticipated. "Well, at the very least, this trip is becoming quite unforgettable." And Charles and I weren't fighting or turning on each other—that was important, too.

He bobbed his head encouragingly. "We'll laugh about it one day."

"Provided we both make it out of here alive," I added gloomily.

"Stop it." Charles brushed a thumb across my cheek. "We'll be just fine. We weren't suspecting any mishaps earlier, but now we're on high alert. We have a plan."

Yes, we had a plan. "I just hope it's the right plan."

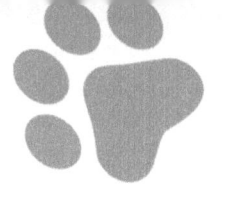

14

We locked the door behind us, and Charles pocketed the key. I carried Charlene out to the garden hidden in the folds of my spare sweater. Thankfully no other guests were lumbering around, leaving me to wonder where they all hung out during the day.

"I think we should start with the bees. I want to ask them if they've seen any other worrying occurrences—things that may be related to the series of misfortunes you've faced since arriving," I explained once I was sure nobody else was around.

Charles dug into his pocket and pulled out a bright yellow tube with an orange cap. "Got my EpiPen, although I should probably teach you how to use it, just in case."

I remained quiet as he talked me through how I could save his life in case of a severe allergic reaction. "I really don't like this," I told him. "It's scary to think of losing you, especially with the kinds of *accidents* that keep happening."

He placed a kiss on my hairline. "You won't lose me. I'll take Charlene to another part of the garden while you speak to the bees. Oh, and while you're talking maybe you can ask them not to sting me?"

"Good idea." Charles headed toward the back of the property with Charlene in tow while I tracked my way back to the yellow roses, knowing the hive was hidden nearby. "Aldrin? Lightyear?" I called out. "Hello, bees? I'd like to talk to you again please."

When nobody responded, I began searching the flowerbeds and trees for any sign of their hive. My search took me farther and farther away from the gorgeous yellow flowers. I finally found a white wooden box hidden in some bushes near the foul-smelling skunk cabbage. "Aldrin? Lightyear?" I tried again with my nose plugged. The cabbage didn't smell nearly as bad today as it had last night, but I still wasn't taking any chances.

"Greetings. How may my colony and I help you, human?" I turned to see an enormously plump bumblebee sitting on a black-eyed Susan nearby.

Given her size and the fact that she was a female, this had to be the queen.

Not knowing the slightest about bee social etiquette, I curtsied—just in case. "Your majesty."

"Please just call me by my name. That shall suffice."

"Yes, your maj—uh, what is your name?"

"I am Bey." *Queen Bey,* of course.

"Hello, Bey. I am Angie. What are you doing out of your hive?" Carefully I lowered myself to the ground and hunched over so that I was closer to eye level with Bey.

She rubbed her front legs together as she spoke. I was now close enough to see that. "My worker drones are hunting for a new location to build our hive. We cannot tolerate being so near this wretched plant."

We both glanced toward the skunk cabbage. "I can't say I blame you there. Do you need my help moving your apiary?"

"No, we will make our own hive, so that the humans can no longer over-harvest our honey. We'll be solving both problems in one action."

I thought of the expression I hated—two birds, one stone—and decided to use a saying I quite liked in its place. "That idea sounds like the bees' knees," I announced proudly and overly amused by myself.

Bey looked down at her plump forelegs, confused. "I do not understand."

I chuckled at her look of bewilderment. "Don't worry about it. Just a silly human expression."

She made a sharp buzzing noise that I took to be a sigh—or maybe a scream. "You may be silly, Angie, but lately other humans have become a danger to us."

"Aldrin and Lightyear told me about the over-harvesting and the new plants," I offered, recalling the earlier conversation.

Bey circled slowly on the flower before settling down again. "Were it not for tradition, we would leave this place altogether. But this lot is where my mother lived out her rule, and her mother before her."

"This garden has sentimental value. I can understand that. What can I do to help ensure you can stay?" I really did want to help. I hadn't spent much time in conversation with bees before now, but I knew from the news that their populations were at risk and that their survival was important to the whole planet. Surely I could do my part to save this one hive while given the chance.

"Keep the other humans away," Bey commanded, her voice haunting. "I do not wish to sacrifice members of my colony to communicate our displeasure via stings. But I fear we are close to that point."

"Oh, yes, that reminds me, please don't sting my husband. He is a good man, and very allergic."

Bey made a strange shrill buzzing sound again. "Sadly, I cannot tell one human from another. I will not even recognize you, should we meet again."

I nodded subtly, not wanting to overdo my motions when speaking with such a tiny creature. "While I have you, then, have you noticed any other strange goings-on in this garden or its house?"

"Strange how?" Bey's voice was growing weak, exhausted. It probably wasn't good for her to spend so long out of the nest. I would be quick with my questions, but first I needed to take a few minutes to catch her up on all the trouble Charles had faced since our arrival.

She sat motionless on the flower, listening with rapt attention. "You humans are a danger to yourselves even more so than us."

I sighed. "That is sadly quite true."

"I can offer no help, other than to tell you much has changed during my reign. These gardens were once the envy of all, but more and more, their glory has been compromised. Not from neglect, but from willful destruction."

"Someone is bringing in the bad plants," I summarized.

"And removing the good ones. Over-harvesting our honey and causing a great famine."

I clucked my tongue at this. "I'm sorry. That's awful."

"We are not the paragon of hard work without reason. Starting today, my workers will be constructing a new hive, and together we will usher in a new era of prosperity. Until then I will endure and put on a strong face for my colony."

"You are a good leader," I assured her.

"As all queens should be."

"Be, ha! Get it, *bees* should *be*?" I couldn't help it. The unexpected pun brightened my mood once more. Hopefully Bey saw the humor in it too.

"You are a strange human, but a kind one. Good luck with your problems."

"Good luck to you with yours. I'll talk with the owner of this house and see if she can offer any help."

"I do not hold out much hope but appreciate your efforts all the same. Farewell, Angie." Queen Bey kept her place on the dark flower center, telling me I had been dismissed from her audience.

Now to find my husband and our temporarily adopted kitten to tell them what little I had learned from our talk—and to see if Charles had any ideas for helping the colony while we were still here at the old stone mansion that held many mysteries within its walls and gardens.

15

We let Charlene prowl around the garden on her own four feet for the next hour, hoping it might encourage mama cat to make contact. We kept close watch to ensure she remained safe and undiscovered by Madame Blue and the other guests.

While she explored, I showed Charles the patch of skunk cabbage and told him how the bees were moving from the apiary to a new self-made hive as a result. "It doesn't smell as bad today, but I'm sure it's still terrible for the bees."

"Let me see here." Charles bent down to examine one of the thick leaves. "Someone trampled it fairly recently. That's probably why it smelled so bad last night but is getting better today."

Shame flooded my chest. "Oh, I hope I wasn't the one to run into it. I'd feel awful for causing all that trouble for Bey and her colony."

"I don't think it was you. Look here." Charles shook his head, then pointed to another section of the cabbage patch. "It's only been flattened in a few spots around the edges. Someone who accidentally ran over it would have left a much more obvious trail."

"So you think someone stomped on it on purpose?" I summarized.

"Well, someone planted it here on purpose," he argued, rising to his feet and then brushing off his palms.

"True. We should probably look around and see if we find anything else that seems out of sorts."

"We can take pictures and reverse image search to figure out the identity of each flower and plant," Charles suggested, pulling out his phone, ready to jump deep down the research rabbit hole. "Perhaps that will be more telling than looking for visual cues."

"Oh, great idea!" I pulled out my phone, too. He and I both loved intellectual challenges, and this was a doozy. "I think there's an app that helps identify flowers too. Let me download it real fast."

For the next hour or so, we took photos of each

plant we found on the lot, trying our best not to attract attention as we catalogued the garden.

"This is tough," I ground out once we'd snapped the last one. "There are so many different sub-species. Like how do we know if this little guy is a Shasta daisy or an ox-eye?" I ran my fingertip over the delicate white flower and sighed.

Charles, however, was still in high spirits. With a focused expression, he tapped on his phone and flipped through a couple articles. "My money's on ox-eye."

"Why?" I leaned over to see what he'd pulled up on his screen.

He handed me the phone while he explained. "It's an invasive species. It looks like a flower, but it's really a weed, famous for destroying the work of inex-perienced gardeners in many climates, including this one."

"But Madame Blue isn't inexperienced," I argued. "When my parents honeymooned here, the garden was perfect, and that was decades ago. Presumably she was the owner then, too."

"My guess is someone swapped the plants out on purpose so that they could destroy the garden from within."

"But who would do that and why?"

Charles shrugged, then joined me in a sigh. "Who would lock me in our room or sabotage the potato salad?"

"I really don't like this." I hung my head, feeling more confused than ever as the clues continued to stack up.

"Me, neither. But I have an idea that should make you feel better."

I looked up, waiting for him to reveal his latest grand idea.

My new husband met me with a loving smile. "Let's call home. I know you've got to be missing everyone there. Talking to them will make you feel better."

"But this week is supposed to be about just us," I argued, shaking my head and grabbing his hand.

He squeezed my hand and then let it go. "I know better than to keep you from your nan. Besides, we'll have the rest of our lives to spend time together just the two of us."

"I like the sound of that," I admitted, biting my lower lip as I thought. "Okay, let's call."

"I'll go find Charlene," he offered, blowing me a kiss as he trounced away.

I wasted no time pulling my phone right back out and placing the call. I really missed my grandmother.

She'd been my best friend as long as I could remember, and it was weird to even go a couple days without seeing her shining face.

She answered my FaceTime call after a few short rings. I couldn't see much of her, but she appeared to be lounging in bed while wearing hot pink silk pajamas and an enormous grin.

"Angie, darling!" she exclaimed, her smile widening even further. "How's married life treating you?"

"Married life is great. I'm not so sure about the rest of it, though," I confessed, trying to keep my expression bright for her benefit.

"I'll be right back, Grant," my grandmother whispered offscreen before returning to me.

"Tell me all about it," she said, moving through the house until she landed in the kitchen. "I'll just put on some tea."

And so I told her everything, concluding with, "But please don't share any of this with Mom or Dad. They were really excited to give us this gift, and I'd hate for them to hear how much trouble this place has been giving us, especially when they both have such fond memories from its heyday.

"Oh, dear. That's terrible," Nan said, steeping a tea bag in a mug of hot water.

"Yeah. I hope your honeymoon is going better than ours?" My words lilted up at the end, seeing as I was almost afraid to ask.

"Well, our honeymoon is next week after you get back. Grant booked a surprise cruise in Alaska!" she gushed, fluffing her hair with one hand like a fancy lady.

I laughed at her show of enthusiasm. You could take the actress off Broadway, but that dramatic persona remained even decades after retirement. "What? Why do you want to go somewhere so cold?" I insisted, now with a genuine smile. Talking to her always made me feel so much better, no matter what else was going on in our lives.

"Oh, *pffft.*" She blew a raspberry, making me giggle. "Grant says they have harsh winters but the most lovely summers in the whole world. We're having a good time here too, though. I never thought I'd remarry after losing your grandfather, but I'm so glad I have Grant now that you're all grown up and starting a family of your own."

"I'm glad you have him, too, but Charles and I are not starting a family just yet," I reminded her with a stern expression.

She waved away my concern with her hand. "You know what I mean, dear."

"I have gotten some unexpected experience with motherhood this week, though." I proceeded to tell her all about Charlene, then added, "Man, you really have missed so much."

"It sounds like it! Many memories in the making, both good and bad, I'd wager." Her eyes held a knowing glint. She and I both knew that some of my worst experiences had turned into my best memories. Like meeting Octo-Cat after my traumatic near-death experience at the hands of a faulty coffee maker.

"That reminds me," I said suddenly, growing excited. "Is Octo-Cat around? Charlene wanted to meet him. She's kind of a fan."

"Uh-oh." Nan's face blanched. "You remember what happened last time that cat had a fan. Pringle entered all of our lives."

"He's not so bad," I said with a smile, remembering the special moment we'd shared on my wedding day.

"Okay. One second, then." The screen grew dark, but I still heard Nan loud and clear. "Paisley, find the kitty!" she shouted in a high-pitched baby voice.

A few moments later, a sharp string of barks rose on the other end of the call. "I think that's my cue," she said with a chuckle, heading up the stairs—not just once, but twice—all the way to my tower bedroom. Charles and I had talked about moving into the master now that he'd be joining me in residence, but I'd become quite attached to my tower.

Apparently, Octo-Cat had, too. Even though he had his own bedroom, complete with a fish tank and everything else a spoiled feline could ever want, he was still hanging out in my room while I was away from home.

While Nan went to get him, I flagged down Charles to tell him I was going inside, then hurried to the privacy of our accommodation.

I'd only just shut the door behind me when Nan held the phone in front of that furry little face I missed so much.

"Aww, what are you doing in my room? Do you miss me?" I cooed, partially teasing but mostly delighted.

His ears pressed down against his head. "Don't be so—"

"I miss you, too," I interrupted so he would know the feeling was mutual. "It's okay to admit you love me, even when nothing bad is going on."

"What do you mean nothing is bad? *Everything* is bad. My Grizabella has gone home, and now I am stuck missing her," he growled as if the whole thing were my fault. To be fair, this was their honeymoon period, too, and they were spending it apart. Despite all our misfortunes, at least Charles and I still had each other.

"I'm really sorry," I said and meant it. "We'll book a trip to go see her in Colorado soon, okay?"

"I'm not okay, but what choice do I have? We can't help who we love, and that darling kitten has my whole heart and soul." He sighed and flopped over onto his side, tail a-swishing.

I think I swooned a little at his declaration of love. Cats—when they showed you love, it was like you became the queen of the whole universe.

As I thought about what I might say next, the door to our room swung open to admit Charles.

I motioned for him to join me on the bed. "Speaking of kittens, there's someone here who would like to meet you," I said, positioning the screen in front of the little black kit-kat.

"So this is my replacement for the week," Octo-Cat intoned, then let out a soft chuff that told me he was just joking.

"Hello, Mr. Octavius. I like your pictures and your story." Charlene appeared unsure of herself as she heaped praises on my tabby back home.

But Octo-Cat ate the praise right up. "The

human's been bragging about me, eh? Can't say I blame her."

"Yes, she loves you very much. And your mate is the most beautiful cat I've ever seen in all my life." Yup, Charlene definitely knew how to get on his good side right from the start.

He smiled wide, teeth and all. "Yeah, kid, you're absolutely right. Hey, Angie, can I talk to you in private for a sec?"

"Sure. Be right back," I told Charles before heading for the communal bathroom and shutting myself inside.

"That kitten is hardly old enough to be away from its mother. What are you doing with her?" he demanded, concern reflecting in his amber eyes.

"She's lost," I explained quietly. "We've been searching for her mother almost non-stop, but so far no luck."

"If you haven't found her yet, she's probably not coming back," he said with eyes lowered, telling me he hated to be the one to deliver this somber news.

"I know, but we have to try."

"Good luck, then. She seems like a sweet kid. I hope it all works out for her."

"Yeah, me too," I said before ending the call.

16

When I returned to our room, I found Charlene bouncing on top of the mattress showing great excitement.

"That was awesome!" she cheered while Charles took a video of her adorable antics.

We really needed to get back outside to look around for her mother some more, but our search was beginning to seem more and more hopeless. And right now the young kitten was so happy that I hated to upset her by abruptly changing the subject. So instead I stood with Charles and watched her celebrate meeting her newfound hero.

When she tired herself out enough to fall back to sleep, we snuggled together while watching a movie on my iPad. Once that was over, Charles ventured into town to grab dinner and some more supplies while I hung back with Charlene, continuing to search local rescue groups for any sign of her lost mother.

That night, we ate dinner in bed, enjoying the simplicity of each other's company. After that, we spent some more time outdoors, hoping Charlene's mother would find us—but no such luck.

We went to bed, the day ending much better than it had started, thanks to our caution. Still, even if we managed to survive the rest of the week at the mansion, we were still facing a ticking clock when it came to reuniting the kitten with her mother. I really hoped this week would have a happy ending for the sweet girl, seeing as Charles and I had already gotten ours.

* * *

I woke up sometime during the night to the sound of heavy footsteps treading outside our door.

Charles slept deeply beside me, his soft breaths making it obvious the sounds hadn't disturbed him in the slightest. Well, that just left me to investigate. I refused to be a sitting duck while someone planted some new trap for us to fall into the next day. Poor

Charles had already been through more than enough.

Tugging my robe around me, I padded out into the dark kitchen and flipped the light switch on.

A shock of rainbow hair greeted me.

"Blaire, what are you doing out here?" I glanced at the digital clock above the stove. "It's two o'clock in the morning!"

"I know what time it is," she told me flatly, shutting the fridge before her, but not without first taking a jug of milk in hand.

"I thought the kitchen was off limits," I pointed out sassily, too tired to try to play nice with someone who wouldn't even meet me halfway.

She rolled her eyes. "Which is why I'm here in the middle of the night, duh."

"You've done this before, haven't you?" I asked as she headed to one of the cupboards and grabbed a glass, seeming to know exactly where she'd find it. "Are you the one who slipped laxatives into the potato salad at lunch?"

Blaire couldn't hide her spurt of laughter, not that she tried to.

"It's not funny," I seethed, then grabbed the glass of milk from her before she could bring it to her lips. "Would you please take this seriously? You poisoned the potatoes, locked him in his room, sabotaged the stairs. When will enough finally be enough?"

Her eyes widened as she ran her fingers over the milk jug's handle. "Calm down. I didn't do any of that, okay? I literally do not care enough about you or your husband to attempt to poison you."

I nervously picked at the skin on my elbow. Was I wrong in accusing Blaire, or was she simply denying her misdeeds now that she'd been caught?

She placed the milk back in the fridge, then asked, "Do you really think someone sabotaged the stairs?"

I nodded emphatically. "Yes, and he could have been seriously injured. In fact, it's basically a miracle that he wasn't."

She frowned, for once showing some small sign of concern for other people's problems. "That's pretty serious. Maybe you should talk to Mademoiselle Blue or whatever her name is."

"But what if she's the one doing all this stuff?" I pointed out in a hushed whisper.

Blaire frowned and shook her head. "No. I mean, why would she?"

"Why would anyone? We know absolutely no one here. None of this makes any sense." I sighed, becoming more and more frustrated as I thought about everything that had transpired since our arrival.

"Why did you think it's me?" Blaire asked, her eyes meeting mine for a second before glancing back toward the counter.

"You're here in the middle of night, right outside our room, and you laughed this morning over the accident on the stairs, then laughed again when I told you about the laxatives."

"Because things like that are funny when they're happening to someone else," she said, rolling her eyes at me a second time.

"It's not funny." I thrust her glass of milk at her, then crossed my arms, incensed. "And for that matter, I still don't know whether I can cross you off the list of suspects. You are here right outside of our room in the middle of the night."

Now Blaire dropped her voice. "It's not what you think, okay?" A pleading expression took over her usually smirking features.

"Then what is it?" I demanded, cocking an eyebrow in question. She could either tell me right now or deal with an increasingly uncomfortable interrogation. I wasn't above tattling to Madame Blue, either.

Blaire must have sensed this because she threw

her hands up in the air and growled. "Ugh, you are so annoying. Do you know that?"

I met her with a deadpan expression, refusing to budge.

"Fine, come with me. I'll show you what I've been hiding."

I followed Blaire upstairs to her second-floor bedroom, which happened to be at least three times larger than the one Charles and I were currently occupying.

She flicked on the lights, then moved across the space to the attached bathroom. "Follow me," she instructed.

I watched as she stooped down by the sink and poured her glass of milk into a China bowl. A flash of movement from the bedroom caught my eye, and I turned just in time to see a black cat racing toward us.

No, not black. *Tortoiseshell.*

"Charlene's mother!" I exclaimed. "You had her this whole time."

The cat turned toward me with wide eyes. "You found my baby?"

At the same time, Blaire asked, "Uh, what? Who's Charlene?"

"Oh, we found an abandoned kitten and decided

to call her Charlene while we searched for her mother," I answered flippantly, trying to hide my screwup.

"What makes you so sure this cat is her mother?" Blaire challenged, eyeing me suspiciously.

"I am her mother! I am! Will you bring her to me?" the torty pleaded, coming over to rub her head against my knee.

I couldn't exactly admit that the kitten had told me and that her cat had just confirmed it to boot. Blaire would think I was crazy, provided she didn't already. I decided to play off her question instead. "I mean, what are the chances of you finding a cat and us finding a kitten so close together?"

"How do you know I found her? What if I brought her here with me?" Blaire was not letting me off the hook.

I just had to meet her confidence with some swagger of my own. "Did you?" I lifted an eyebrow.

"No, but that's not the point. You're making a lot of assumptions here. Just like you assumed I did all that stuff to your husband."

"Okay, I get your point, but something tells me this is the kitten's mom. They're both mostly black, if that helps prove anything. Can I bring the kitten up here to introduce her? We should know by how they interact if they belong together."

"Yes, yes! I want to see my Charlene!" the torty cried, now pawing at my knee enthusiastically. "I've missed her so much!"

Blaire just shrugged, completely oblivious to the pleas of her new feline friend. "I guess. If it will get you off my back," she said, and I rushed out of there to grab the kitten before the rainbow-haired woman could change her mind.

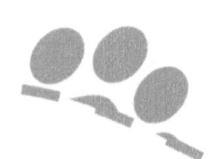

17

returned to the room and flipped the light on to help me find Charlene more easily than groping about in the dark. Charles still didn't stir even from the bright flood of light—sleeping off all the drama of the day, no doubt.

"Charlene," I whispered when I didn't immediately spot her. "We found your mother. C'mon."

The little kitten jolted out from beneath my abandoned pillow. "Really? Let's go!" she squeaked happily.

"You've got it, boss." I scooped her up, turned out the light, and jogged back up the secondary staircase to reach Blaire's room upstairs.

As soon as I'd returned, the mother cat came running. Even before I could set Charlene on the floor, she was pawing at my legs and shouting, "My baby! My baby!"

"Mommy!" Charlene mewled in matching excitement. "It's really you!"

Blaire stood back and watched this happy reunion from the bathroom doorway. "Okay, so they probably do belong to each other," she admitted. "I wasn't planning on keeping two cats, but I guess it's fine."

"You're keeping Charlene's mother?" I asked, not sure why I hadn't pieced that together already but still surprised all the same.

"Her name is Socks," Blaire corrected, creeping over to join me and the cats.

"That's not my name," the mother said as she busily groomed Charlene with her sandpaper tongue. "But I don't mind."

"Why Socks?" I wanted to know. I supposed most pets had their names changed by humans once adopted, but this one made zero sense. "She doesn't have any. Her feet are all black."

Blaire smirked at my question. "That's the point. It's ironic. *Duh.*"

"Well, then hello, Socks." I ran my hand over the tortoiseshell cat's back, and she lifted her tail happily.

"Charlene is a dumb name. I'm changing it," Blaire said a few seconds later.

Neither cat seemed to pay her much mind as she ran through a list of possible names. "I think I'll call her Snowball," she landed on after at least a dozen such *ironic* possibilities. "And don't you dare point out that she's not white. That's the whole point."

Stupid names aside, Blaire did seem committed to the feline mother-daughter duo. Still, something nagged at me. "You'll take good care of them, right?"

She seemed offended by my innocent question. "Of course I will," she practically snarled at me.

I said nothing, focusing my attention on Charlene. This was really goodbye, and I couldn't even talk with her properly while Blaire was watching. I'd sure miss the little fluff ball, but she got what she'd wanted this whole time, and she would have a home, too. I felt much better, knowing she'd be off the streets.

"I guess I should let you all get back to sleep." I pushed myself back to my feet, hesitant to leave but also knowing it was for the best. "We have some supplies for Charl—um, Snowball—in our room. I'll bring them by in the morning. Let me know if you need anything else by then, okay? Charles and I will probably be checking out to grab a hotel in town."

She perked up instantly. "On account of someone trying to kill your husband?"

"I don't know about *kill,* but yes. We don't exactly feel safe here."

"Well, at least you have somewhere to go. I have two cats and no home." She glanced up at me with tear-rimmed eyes, an unexpected display of emotion from the mostly stoic girl. "Dylan and I broke up today. I'm only staying here until the old lady realizes I can't pay and kicks me out."

My heart went out to her, especially since I was in the exact opposite predicament. I was literally here celebrating my honeymoon. "Do you need some money, Blaire?" I offered gently.

She snorted. "I need a job. I met Dylan at work, so naturally I quit. I can't stand the thought of having to see him every single day. It would be too awkward."

"Well, I'm sure something will turn up." My well-intended optimism was not well-received.

"Okay, Boomer," she practically barked. "I'll just walk into an office and immediately land my dream job without so much as an interview, then I'll get a mortgage on a three-bedroom house by batting my eyelashes and promising not to default. All I'll need after that is a white picket fence, and I can live happily ever after. I'll pass on the whole Prince Charming facade, thanks."

Okay, that was pretty harsh.

"I am nowhere near old enough to be a Boomer." I tried to keep the upset from my voice, seeing as the girl was having a rough time already. "But I have a good feeling about your future, even if you don't."

With that, I left.

Charlene was so caught up in the reunion with her mother, she didn't even see me go. Oh, well. It was for the best, right? Even if Blaire had nothing else, she would at least have the love of two very special felines.

I trudged slowly toward the staircase, trying to come to terms with how I was feeling in that moment. For the last day and a half, Charles and I had been focused almost solely on finding the missing mother cat, and now that we had... I was really going to miss that kitten.

Maybe I was more prepared to be a mother than I originally thought. Or maybe I just really liked cats.

Who knew?

Certainly not me.

I paused to look out at the garden from the window beside the secondary staircase and was startled to spy movement outside. I squinted in an attempt to clarify the picture, but it was all so dark.

Past midnight was no time to work in the garden. Could whatever was happening out there somehow be related to all the trouble Charles and I had been facing since our arrival? Was that the guilty party right outside the window already working to sabotage us yet again?

I honestly didn't know, but I certainly had to go out there to take a closer look.

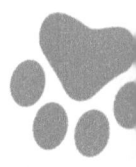

18

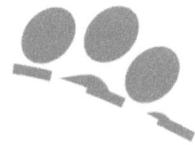

This time I did wake Charles. It took several good shakes, but finally his eyes blinked open.

"What time is it?" he groaned, covering his eyes to block out the light.

"Late," I confessed with an apologetic wince. "I'm sorry. It's just I found Charlene's mother, and now there's something going on in the garden. I'd feel safer if you were with me."

He struggled to sit up in bed. "You found Charlene's mother?" This was followed by a sharp gasp of pain.

"Oh, sweetie." I reached over to rub his shoulders.

He leaned into my touch. "I guess that fall hurt

me more than I initially realized. Let me just pop a couple Tylenol and—"

"It's okay. You should rest." And I should have known better than to wake him. Of course he was putting on a strong face after that horrid accident. He didn't want to worry me, and now I'd only made things worse by disturbing him while his body was trying to heal.

He shrugged off my concern and practically leapt out of bed, as if to prove a point. "And miss the action? No way."

I waited as he swallowed a couple capsules dry.

He clapped his hands together to signal his readiness to proceed. "Let's go see what's happening. And after that, you'll tell me about finding Charlene's mother?"

"Definitely. I can even take you to meet her in the morning, but I don't know how much longer that person will be outside."

Charles locked the door behind us, then shot me a worried glance. "A person is out there? Doing what?"

"I don't know. That's what I want to find out."

"Fair enough," was the last thing either of us said before quietly moving through the house and very quietly letting ourselves outside.

We held hands as we moved toward the dark

figure to get a better look. The sound of a shovel breaking the soil rang out through the night.

"What was that? Do you think someone's burying a body?" I whispered, fear surging through my body.

"I think..." Charles said, leaning down to whisper in my ear. "That my wife needs to stop watching so many true crime documentaries."

"Who's there?" a man called into the chilly night air. Apparently, we hadn't been quiet enough. I blamed our extreme sleepiness for us being careless enough to get discovered in our covert spy operation almost immediately.

Charles let go of my hand and moved in front of me to shield me from the stranger. "We were just coming out for some fresh air," he announced, creeping closer with me behind him.

"Who are you, and what are you doing here?" I shouted, my voice quaking.

The man clicked on a flashlight and shone it beneath his face, creating a ghoulish affect. "It's me, Bill."

"Gardening at night a habit of yours?" Charles's voice was light and airy, conversational. He was an expert at questioning witnesses and suspects alike.

"Usually, no, but there was no time during the day, what with the fiasco on the stairs and all the room switching. Tomorrow will be another busy day, so I figured I'd just knock this out now, before the old lady realized I'd fallen behind on my chores." He took a step back, releasing a familiar foul smell into the air.

"Is that skunk cabbage?" I asked, immediately moving to pinch my nose.

Billy swept his flashlight toward the freshly planted cabbage. About half the gorgeous yellow roses had been uprooted to make way for their highly undesirable replacement, and this made me quite sad. The bees loved those roses and were likely planning on constructing their new hive nearby. Now the same plant that had driven them from their apiary would ruin this new location, too.

"Why would you tear up flowers and plant skunk cabbage in their place?" Charles asked, sounding genuinely curious. I knew him well enough, though, to see that he was just two steps away from levying a serious accusation the porter's way.

"It's all these darned bees," Billy complained, lifting a hand to wipe sweat from his brow. "They're scaring the guests. Madame Blue suspects they're to blame for our lack of return bookings. She needed the money, so she wants them out of here. Obviously we can't kill them, so I'm trying to drive them away using more natural means."

"But you're ruining the garden in the process," I argued, protective of the place where we'd spent so much time over the last couple of days, the place my parents still remembered so fondly from decades past.

Billy swung his flashlight toward the uprooted roses. "These guys? Nah. I'll move them to pots for the time being, then return them to this soil once the bees have left. No harm, no foul."

Except this was incredibly harmful to the bees. They would be forced to leave their ancestral land, just because Madame Blue didn't realize her unfriendly staff and deteriorating house were the real reasons so many guests never returned.

Charles and I, for one, couldn't wait to get out of there.

19

The next morning, Charles and I were up early despite our strange night-time excursion. He was excited to visit Charlene and her mother so we could all say goodbye before we packed up and headed to a nice, safe, *boring* hotel chain in town. I would take boring all day long if it kept my husband from facing any more misplaced misfortunes.

The only problem was that we had no idea what time Blaire might wake up, and I didn't want to be the one to roust the cranky young adult from her sleep. So Charles and I busied ourselves by grabbing showers in the communal bathroom and packing up our luggage. When that was done, we scarfed down some protein bars that Charles had picked up on his latest supply run.

"After this, it's only the finest Southern dining for the rest of the week," he promised, pulling me into his side for a snuggle.

"Laxative-free, too, right?" I joked before offering him a peck on the cheek. He needed a shave, but I also liked this laidback vacation version of my new husband. The scruff made him appear even more handsome. Maybe I could convince him to grow out a beard.

He dropped a hand to his stomach in memory. "Ugh. I sure hope so."

I quirked a brow. "Too soon?"

"No, it's just..." His words fell away. "Did you hear that?"

Both of us directed our gazes toward the closed door, where the sounds of soft but persistent scratching rose to meet our ears, then suddenly fell away.

"Do you think it could be Charlene?" I asked, filled with joy at the thought. I assumed we'd have to wait at least another couple hours to see Blaire and the cats, but maybe I was wrong.

Charles was grinning like a maniac, too. "Only one way to find out."

We both moved swiftly toward the door. Charles was the one to pry it open. When we looked down, however, nothing was there.

"What is this?" Madame Blue shouted from a couple paces away, holding our kitten up by the scruff of her neck.

Charlene twisted and writhed but couldn't break free. I stomped right over to them and grabbed Charlene from the horrid old woman's clutches. "Why are you so mean?" I demanded.

"You knew the rules. No pets allowed!" she huffed.

"She's not a pet. She's just a poor lost kitten who got separated from her mother."

The sound of footsteps stomping down the stairs diverted everyone's attention before Madame Blue could offer a rejoinder. We all turned to see Blaire racing toward us rather breathlessly.

"There you are, Snowball!" she cried, stopping to rest against the counter.

"Is this your pet?" Madame Blue insisted.

"Yes," Blaire claimed, proudly raising her chin in defiance.

"No pets allowed," the old woman shouted, her face growing red.

"Oops," was all Blaire said before taking the kitten from my protective arms.

Madame Blue huffed, apparently unsure of how to respond to Blaire's complete inability to care.

Charlene squirmed in Blaire's arms and turned to face me and Charles. "I'm sorry if I caused trouble. I was coming to find you. I missed you!" she mewled sadly.

My heart broke for her, but I was also still incredibly livid.

"What happened?" Blaire mused, stroking the kitten in her arms as she faced the woman. "Cat got your tongue?"

"Young lady, I will not be disrespected in my own home!" the proprietress fumed.

"Yet you disrespect all your guests constantly. That's why we're leaving," I shot in, hands on my hips in a power pose. "Ever since we got here, it's been one problem after another. You don't even care that my husband fell through the stairs due your negligence in keeping up the property. You forced us to change rooms, locked him into the bedroom, slipped laxatives into the potato salad. And to top it all off, you hate animals, first with the bees and now with this sweet kitten."

The old woman blinked several times hard. "What a string of accusations! All false, of course."

"Really? Then maybe you should explain yourself," Charles urged from my side. His voice was much calmer than mine, which I guess made me the bad cop in this scenario.

Blue placed her hands on the counter to steady herself, her voice shaking with rage that matched my own. "I have the house appraised every five years so that nothing falls into disrepair. The stairs were fine as of our last inspection about two years back, so that accident was not on behalf of my negligence. I've practically bankrupted myself keeping this house to code to appease the historical society. As for getting locked in the room, old doors stick sometimes. These are the originals after all, and I came and helped you out just as soon as I got back that day. And my cooking? How dare you insult my cooking to accuse me of putting laxatives in the potatoes, when the rest of us ate them and were just fine. Maybe you have traveler's diarrhea, I don't know, but again, not my fault. I already explained why pets aren't allowed. This is a place of business and it's my right to make the rules. What if a guest was deathly allergic, huh?"

"What about the bees, then?" I challenged,

prompted by her comment on allergies, which made me realize she hadn't addressed that part yet. "Why would you intentionally drive them from the property?"

Madame Blue appeared quite taken aback by this. She even literally took one step back as if she'd been slapped. "I am not trying to drive the bees away. I love them. I use their honey in my tea every morning and had planned to expand this dying business by selling their honey at the local farmer's market. It's why I was at the bank that day, trying to get a loan. I hate dealing with ungrateful, self-important guests, but I love those bees."

"Then why are you planting skunk cabbage and ox-tail daisies and other things that will choke out the garden?" Charles wanted to know. I admired how calm he was able to remain. It was probably the only reason Madame Blue was willing to explain herself at all.

"I am not doing any of that! The garden is my pride and joy, but ever since I took a spill last winter, I haven't been able to get around as well as I used to. That all falls to Billy now."

"We saw Billy last night, close to three a.m.," Charles revealed. "He was outside digging up the roses and replacing them with skunk cabbage. He said it's what you wanted because the bees were scaring off the guests."

We all watched Blue for her reaction, which was one of genuine shock.

"He couldn't possibly have said that. It's not true!" she insisted, shaking her head emphatically.

Charles sighed. "Perhaps you better take a look in the garden, then."

After that, we marched outside, Blaire and Charlene in tow, and together Charles and I pointed out the spots where skunk cabbage had been both planted and systematically trampled. We also showed her the place where daisies had been swapped for a lookalike invasive species.

"I can't believe any of this," Madame Blue said in a jarringly quiet voice. It was the first time since our arrival two days back that any of her words hadn't been yelled.

"Looks like Billy has some explaining to do," Blaire said with a smirk before setting her phone to record video. That girl lived for the drama.

Me? I just wanted a happy resolution for all involved, especially the bees who depended on this garden for their livelihood.

I couldn't wait to hear what Billy had to say for himself.

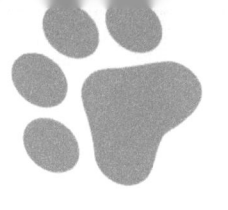

20

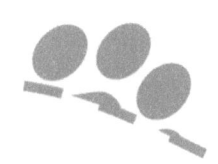

We marched in a straight line to the third floor of that old stone mansion.

"Billy! Get out here right this instant!" Madame Blue yelled through a closed door.

He grumbled something I couldn't quite make out, then pried the door open, seeming to have forgotten to put on a shirt. "What is it? I don't start work for another hour, and you know that," he complained. His eyes grew wide as he saw the entourage that joined his employer—me, Charles, Charlene, Blaire, and Blaire's phone, already recording.

"Let me put on a shirt," he muttered, shutting the door on us.

We all waited in silence until the door popped

back open and Billy ushered us in. His room was small, just like the new one we'd been moved to on the first floor. It felt incredibly crowded with all five of us standing in the space, but nobody wanted to leave before getting answers.

"Well?" Billy demanded with a snide expression on his grizzled face. "What's so important that it couldn't wait one hour?"

The old lady marched right up to him and poked him in the chest with her finger. "What's this I hear about skunk cabbage and bees?"

"What about it?" Billy answered smoothly. "You asked me to find a way to get rid of the bees, so I opted for a natural method."

"I did not ask you to get rid of the bees!" Madame Blue stomped her foot in frustration. "You and I both know how much those bees mean to me."

Billy's featured pinched. "But you did ask me, Bluebell. Why else would I try to drive them off?"

"Lies!" the old woman hissed.

"Not lies," Billy countered calmly. "Let me get dressed, and I can drive you into town to see your doctor. We both knew this day was coming."

"If you're trying to suggest I'm senile, you've got another think coming. My hips are bad, hearing's gone, but my memory is just fine. I did not ask you to scare off my honeybees."

They both seemed so sure of their position, it was hard to know who was telling the truth.

"Knock, knock," someone called from out in the hall. Before anyone could answer, Madeline Mackenzie let herself into the room. She was wearing yet another Hawaiian shirt. How many did this woman have in her wardrobe?

"I heard shouting and just wanted to make sure everything was all right." She shot Billy a meaningful glance, and that's when it all clicked into place.

"You!" I rounded her, pointing a finger in accusation. "You're the one who caused all those accidents. You locked my husband in our room, and I'm willing to bet you messed with the stairs, too."

"That's ridic—"

"The game is up, Madeline," Billy interjected, obvious relief coloring his expression. "Just admit what you did."

Everyone waited for someone to confess, but nobody did.

"You wanted the house for yourselves," I explained. "You were willing to do anything to get it, including endangering the other guests."

"Silly and offensive!" Mrs. Mackenzie shouted.

I came right up to her and poked my finger into her chest, same as Blue had done with Billy. "And true!" Now we were all shouting.

"I didn't do any of those things," she fumed, crossing her arms over her chest.

"Okay, can you prove that you didn't?" Charles posed calmly.

She growled but didn't respond with any words.

"I think maybe I can," Blaire said, coming forward with phone in hand. She handed it to me.

"You know how I've been sneaking around at night to take things from the kitchen? I didn't put two and two together before, but look at this." Blaire hit play on the video, and my eyes grew wide as I watched the scene unfold. She'd managed to catch footage of Mrs. Mackenzie and Billy meeting by the broken staircase before it had been broken.

"They didn't see me, and I thought this was some kind of midnight lovers thing despite the obviously enormous age gap."

"Why would you record that?"

She shrugged. "I record everything. Thought this would either turn funny, disgusting, or into good blackmail fodder. Since I didn't have money to keep staying here, I thought maybe I could convince one of them to foot the bill in exchange for me keeping their secret. I just hadn't hit that point of desperation yet."

I watched as they talked for a while, pointed at the stairs, talked some more, then hugged and wandered off in separate directions.

"What were they saying?" I asked, confused as to how this was the smoking gun we needed.

"Just stuff about plans and being ready. Again, I thought it was about an affair, but maybe they were plotting something else. Maybe they were working together to sabotage your stay."

Neither Billy nor Mrs. Mackenzie said anything in response to this accusation. That's when Mr. Mackenzie joined us.

"What's all this talk of having an affair?" he asked good-naturedly, clearly thinking it was out of the realm of possibilities.

"We think—" I started, but Blaire cut us off.

"Sorry to be the one to break it to you, but your wife is cheating on you with that guy!" Blaire pointed to Billy.

He looked from his wife to Billy, then burst out laughing. "No way. That's our son. Didn't you know?"

"What?" Madame Blue shouted. "How come nobody said anything to me?"

"I guess it slipped our minds," Mrs. Mackenzie said with a wave of her hand.

"Or you didn't want her to know," I suggested, unmoved by this shock twist. If anything, it made the pieces fit together more perfectly. "How long ago did you hire Billy to help out around here?" I asked Madame Blue.

"About two years ago. Why?"

"That was after your most recent inspection, right?"

"Just a couple months after, yes. It was the enormity of the repairs needed that made me realize I couldn't do it all on my own anymore."

"Madame Blue, you're not losing your memory. You've been double-crossed," I revealed dramatically.

"Of course I'm not losing my memory. I'm sharp as a tack, but what do you mean about double-crossed?"

"These two"—I pointed at the mother and son—"were working together to sabotage your business. She has a special place in her heart for the house but can't buy unless you put it for sale. Billy has been her inside man. He's been secretly damaging the house, ruining the gardens, and encouraging guests to leave bad reviews," I added thinking back to how nonchalant he was while we were changing rooms, even going so far as to suggest we leave negative feedback online. "Scaring off the bees was probably meant to be the last straw, since you love them so much. He thought that you'd have no reason to stay with everything that was going wrong."

Mr. Mackenzie did not look happy about any of this. "These are very serious accusations you're making."

"Yet somehow they're true."

"You can't prove anything," Billy said flatly.

"Well, my friend, you messed with the wrong guests," I said with a smirk of my own. "My husband's a lawyer and I'm a private investigator."

"And I record almost everything," Blaire added.

"I'm sure with a little digging we could piece together a timeline of events, uncover receipts for repairs that never happened, and even get a clean bill of health from Madame Blue's doctor to prove her memory is just fine."

"We should get another inspector in too. To check out the stairs and see if there's been any obvious tampering."

"There's no need to do that," Mrs. Mackenzie said. "We'll leave. That's what you wanted, right? You want the good room back?"

"This is about so much more than a room."

"Did you really do what they're saying, Madeline? Billy?" Mr. Mackenzie asked with a crestfallen expression. "I know we wanted this place, but we all agreed to wait until the old woman died. Goodness knows that should happen soon enough."

"Billy, you're fired," Madame Blue growled. "Get off my property."

"Before you go." Charles stepped forward with a business card in hand. "I'll be representing Madame Blue in a suit to reclaim damages due to willful destruction of property. Expect a call from me soon."

EPILOGUE
FOUR DAYS LATER

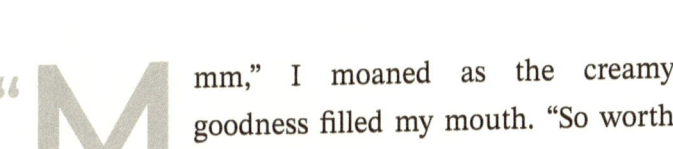

"Mmm," I moaned as the creamy goodness filled my mouth. "So worth the wait."

"Cheers to that," Charles said, holding up his fork to bump it to mine as the sun rose over the garden.

"Ready for another round?" Madame Blue asked, hovering nearby with a Pyrex dish half-filled with the delicious homemade biscuits and gravy.

"We should save some for Blaire," I suggested, daintily wiping at the corners of my mouth as if I weren't making a huge mess of myself already. "She'll be hungry when she finishes replanting those roses."

This was the last day of our stay at the old stone mansion so beloved by my parents. Now that Billy and his parents had gone, it was a perfectly lovely place to vacation. The inspector had come out yesterday to assess the house and its property. We were still waiting on an official report, but he noted at least sixty thousand dollars' worth of new damages since the last inspection.

Charles had wasted no time in letting the Mackenzies know that they were expected to pay for all the damages in duplicate—or he would file a suit over the accident he'd suffered on the tampered staircase, and he would be sure to win.

Madame Blue still needed the help, of course, and since Blaire still needed a home, the two decided to help each other. And Blaire was already teaching her new employer all about how social media could help her increase bookings. They'd even submitted a listing to AirBnB and already had a couple stays booked for later in the month.

It seemed to be a match made in heaven.

Blaire's only request was that Socks be allowed to stay on the premises, despite the no pets rule.

Just Socks.

Charlene would be coming home with us.

It turns out our time spent helping her led to all of us being quite attached, which is why she'd snuck out of Blaire's room to come find us.

"I love my mommy, but I'm old enough to be on

my own now. Or at least to be with you," Charlene had said when she asked us to become her family.

Socks also gave her approval. "It's what cats do, and it's a mother's greatest delight to know her child is truly happy in life. Thank you for loving my sweet baby."

And that was that.

"Her name being so much like mine was a sign," Charles said. "We always belonged together."

I liked that, and I hoped Octo-Cat, Jacques, and Jillianne would be accepting of the new baby when we brought her home, further blending our household. Now we had my cat, Charles's cats, and one that was both of ours. Soon I hoped we would be a cohesive family unit, but these things took time... especially when cats were involved.

"Ready for a break?" Madame Blue shouted across the yard.

Blaire stood and tore off the oversized gardening gloves. "I'm starving," she said before striding over to join us.

"You didn't have to wake up so early for our benefit," I reminded her.

"Maybe not, but I wanted to make sure to see you off before you left," she said with a smile. Yes, Blaire visibly liked me now. I considered it one of my greatest achievements from this week.

"When is the apiarist coming by again?" Madame Blue asked. Now that she would be receiving a generous stipend from the Mackenzies, she had enough cash to expand operations, just as she'd always wanted. The apiarist would be consulting on a new bee house and inspecting the current colony so they could talk about how best to introduce even more bees to the lot.

Queen Bey's reign would be one for the history books. You know, if bees had history books.

"Did you have a good week?" Charles asked just as we were about to climb into the car and head back to Maine, Charlene in tow.

"The best," I answered before we shared one final kiss. "I can see why Mom and Dad like it so much."

"Me, too." Charles smiled and let out a wistful sigh. "We should come back for our first anniversary. Just eleven months and some change to go."

"I can't wait," I answered with one last look back at the enchanting stone mansion where we'd made so many memories.

"Bye, Mommy!" Charlene shouted happily, and with that, it was time to move on to our next adventure.

. . .

All good things must come to an end, and the next adventure will be the gang's last. How does the story end before they all ride off into the sunset to enjoy their literary retirement?

You won't want to miss this one!

Get your copy of *Animal Accomplice,* so that you can keep reading this series today!

* * *

Pssst... If you absolutely loved this book and want even more, make sure you **sign up for Molly's newsletter**. When you do, you'll receive an exclusive digital prize pack, including a free book!

WHAT'S NEXT?

The jig is up. Someone knows my secret.

What starts as mild online harassment soon turns much more dire when my blackmailer reveals irrefutable proof of my ability to talk to animals, promising to expose me whether I like it or not.

I've always lived life on my own terms, but if word were to get out about my secret superpower, I know better than anyone that things would never be the same... for me or anyone I love.

With the stakes higher than ever, Octo-Cat and I decide to take on one last case. First we must reveal the identity of my anonymous bully, and then we'll have to ask ourselves the hardest question yet: Where do we go from here?

ANIMAL ACCOMPLICE is now available.

Get your copy so that you can keep reading this zany mystery series today!

SNEAK PEEK
ANIMAL ACCOMPLICE

My name is Angie Longfellow, and I lead a pretty great life. For the longest time, I had trouble finding my path, racking up associate degrees and building my resume like nobody's business.

I never would have suspected my crummy job as a paralegal for the local law firm would have led to my happily ever after, but it brought me both my husband and my very special, *very secret* ability.

So, yeah, I can talk to animals, a fact that more or less rules my day-to-day life.

It all started when a faulty coffee maker zapped me unconscious at a will reading, only for me to be awoken by the deceased's cat—who also just so happened to be her primary beneficiary. With vile tuna breath, he informed me that his old lady had not died of natural causes and that it was up to me to help him solve the murder and bring her killer to justice.

At first I could only talk to him—to Octo-Cat—but now I can talk to pretty much any animal or insect that is willing to talk back. My regular entourage includes that original talking tabby, my husband's two hairless cats Jacques and Jillianne, our newly adopted kitten Charlene, and Pringle the raccoon who lives in a swanky set of tree houses in the backyard.

Paisley the rescue Chihuahua moved out when Nan went to live with her new husband Grant. I miss having her in the house, but I still see her nearly every day, along with Grant's rescue bunny—a Holland Lop named E.B.

It's strange not living with my grandmother anymore, but I do love married life. Charles works long hours as the senior partner at the law firm, and I don't have much to do, given that my P.I. business rarely has any clients.

So in the meantime, Nan is teaching me to be domestic. I'm pretty good at cleaning the house, but my cooking leaves much to be desired. Still, I have a lot of time to figure things out since Charles works such long hours.

To fill my time, I also read several books per week, which is kind of a dream come true. Except it's starting to wear on me.

I love reading about others' adventures—don't get me wrong—but I also want to live my own. I was the main character here, not some simple spectator. Lately, though, my life doesn't have a whole lot of plot.

Strange how having all your dreams come true can turn out to be so boring. It's like I have nothing left to strive for, that I already have everything I've ever wanted—and then some.

Between Charles's cushy paycheck and Octo-Cat's trust fund, we're more than covered financially, but still, I'd like to make my business a success for my own satisfaction.

There's just two problems with that. First, Nan and my mom took it upon themselves to register my firm with the state government as Pet Whisperer P.I., which means I'm stuck with the name. Second, I'm not the sole owner. Octo-Cat is my partner, and he's not always the easiest to work with.

In fact, he doesn't want to do any work at all, not

since he piggybacked on my wedding to marry his long-time, long-distance girlfriend, Grizabella, the former show cat. Then right after that, we subsequently adopted Charlene, the little lost kitten Charles and I found on our honeymoon.

Now our Octavius is a full-time doting dad and a constant critic of yours truly. I have a feeling *that* will never change, no matter how much I might want it to.

* * *

"You're slouching," Octo-Cat growled shortly after entering our shared office.

I straightened my spine then let out a long, frustrated sigh and clicked my laptop shut. Twisting in my desk chair, I turned to face my feline partner. "Where's Charlene?" I asked with one eyebrow quirked in question.

Octo-Cat sat and idly licked at a paw. "The nudists have her for late-morning classes."

"I really wish you'd stop calling the Sphynx cats that." I groaned. Still, I found it adorable that the three cats had rallied around our new arrival, even going so far as to homeschool her. I had no idea what they taught her during these catting lessons, but everyone seemed more or less content, so I didn't pry.

He dropped his paw to the ground and stared at me with wide amber eyes. "Do you prefer I go back to referring to them as the interlopers?"

"But you're all getting along now," I argued, drumming my fingers on my knee as I thought about how I might turn this conversation around before my kitty partner became too agitated.

He just shook his head. "Thus the new nickname. You can't deny the fact they're naked, Angela. If they wanted to grow fur, they would have done it by now."

I chose not to acknowledge that with anything more than an exacerbated eye roll.

Octo-Cat shifted his eyes toward the desk then back to me in the chair. Thankfully, it was he who changed the subject, although it was definitely one I didn't care for. "Are you really done with work already? It's hardly past breakfast time."

"I'm just not making any progress, and I feel bad spending Charles's money when the ads clearly aren't working."

"You never felt bad about spending my money," he pointed out with a holier-than-thou expression.

Heat rushed to my cheeks. "That was different," I

admitted, glancing down at my lap before returning my gaze to him in embarrassment.

"Oh?" Octo-Cat tilted his head to the side as he studied me. "Then go ahead. Please do tell me how."

"Well, you're my business partner, and it's not exactly like you work for your income," I mumbled meekly; my confidence could never match his and that often became a problem.

The tabby scoffed at this. "I don't work? Ha. Is that so? I'll have you know that I work very hard keeping tabs on you all day."

I pressed both palms to my thighs and then stood. "Look, I'm not trying to start a fight or anything. I'm just feeling discouraged is all."

"I already told you. You've been doing the work for free for far too long. Nobody wants to pay for it now."

I sighed. Octo-Cat was a pretty good sleuth, but he was a terrible businessman. I wasn't much better, but I still knew I could learn. My cat seemed to think he was infallible in this and all things.

I stopped at the door and turned back to him. "It's not that—"

"Not to mention, the one time you did have a paying client, you pinned the crime on him!" he shouted as if it were the silliest thing he'd ever heard.

"He was guilty," I argued right back. Frankly, I was done with this conversation, but I knew Octo-Cat wouldn't drop it until he was satisfied, meaning I was stuck for the moment. "Was I supposed to turn a blind eye just because he was paying us?"

My cat shrugged. "It was a bad business decision. That's all I'm saying."

Was my cat right? Was I hopeless at this whole business thing? Well, it wasn't like I could go out and find another private investigation firm to hire me on salary. This kind of work was pretty much freelance, which meant if I wanted to continue as a detective, I'd have to get a whole lot better at the business side. *Ugh*. Perhaps it was time to simply admit defeat. All my other dreams had come true, so why did I continue to cling to the only one that hadn't?

"Maybe I should ask Charles for some paralegal work," I admitted with a sigh. "I was good at that. Plus, having something to do with myself would make it so I don't feel quite so useless."

My cat growled at me. "You are not leaving me here alone all day. What if I need fresh water? What if someone comes to the door? What then, Angela?"

I ignored him and headed down the hall in the direction of the grand staircase. Perhaps I'd feel better about this whole failed businesswoman thing once I'd had a bit of lunch.

Was ten a.m. too early for my second meal of the day?

ANIMAL ACCOMPLICE is now available.

Get your copy so that you can keep reading this zany mystery series today!

ABOUT MOLLY FITZ

While *USA Today bestselling* author Molly Fitz can't technically talk to animals, she and her three feline writing assistants have deep and very animated conversations as they navigate their days.

She lives with her child and their own private zoo somewhere in the wilds of Alaska. Molly will occasionally venture out for good food, great coffee, or to meet new animal friends.

Learn more about Molly and her books, and be sure to sign up for her newsletter at **www.MollyMysteries.com**.

ALSO BY MOLLY FITZ

Learn more about Molly's collected works, so that you can decide which book you'd like to read next...

PET WHISPERER P.I.

Angie Russo just partnered up with Blueberry Bay's first ever talking cat detective. Along with his ragtag gang of human and animal helpers, Octo-Cat is determined to save the day... so long as it doesn't interfere with his schedule.

Start with book 1, ***Kitty Confidential***.

MERLIN'S MAGICAL MYSTERIES

Gracie Springs is not a witch... but her cat is. Now she must help to keep his secret or risk spending the rest of her life in some magical prison. Too bad trouble seems to find them at every turn!

Start with book 1, ***Merlin Takes a Familiar***.

PARANORMAL TEMP AGENCY

Tawny Bigford's simple life takes a turn for the magical when she stumbles upon her landlady's murder and is recruited by a talking black cat named Fluffikins to take over the deceased's role as the official Town Witch for Beech Grove, Georgia.

Start with book 1, ***Witch for Hire***.

THE MYSTERIES OF MOONLIGHT MANOR (WITH TRIXIE SILVERTALE)

Sydney Coleman has it all—until she doesn't. No sooner does she launch her bed and breakfast, than a trio of ghosts turn up oppose her at every turn. They insist she solve the murder of their mistress, but Sydney is desperate for cash. If she can't book some guests fast, her haunted mansion is utterly doomed.

Start with book 1, ***Moonlight & Mischief***.

CONNECT WITH MOLLY

Sign up for my newsletter and get a special digital prize pack for joining, including an exclusive story, *Meowy Christmas Mayhem*, fun quiz, and lots of cat pictures!

Sign up: **MollyMysteries.com/subscribe**

Now, if you ever wished you could converse with cats, here's your opportunity! This is me officially inviting you into my whacky inner world as part of my Cozy Kitty Book Club.

For those who just can't get enough of my zany cat characters and their hapless humans, this book club will provide new content to devour and the chance to get to know my best author friends.

From exclusive stories, behind-the-scenes trivia to never-before-released bonus content, and monthly giveaways, there's a lot to love about the Cozy Kitty

Book Club. Join today to find out what we're reading next!

Join: **MollyMysteries.com/club**